HIJINKS & MURDER

A VIOLET CARLYLE HISTORICAL COZY

BETH BYERS

SUMMARY

January 1926

Violet has received an obscure note, a strange request, and the claim of a murder. She'd like to ignore it, but the writer knows too much about her.

Has someone been murdered? Who is the author of the note and why are they dragging Violet into this crime? Just what is going on and will Violet be able to reach the bottom of this madness?

CHAPTER 1

"$\mathcal{D}$arling," Violet told Jack as she turned onto her side. "Do you realize that Lila and Denny are having a baby?"

He laughed at her, but it was with an edge of wondering if she was going to suggest that they too have a baby. He wasn't against children, but neither of them felt all that ready to have one. If anything, Jack's recent wound in the line of duty made Violet even less willing to have a child.

She grinned at him, cupping his cheek and letting her thumb run along his jaw as she added, "Victor and Kate seem to not understand how to... not have babies—" Her twin brother and his wife had very young twins of their own, and Kate was expecting again. Given that Kate got so ill during pregnancy, they were both essentially housebound.

Jack snorted at that, turning onto his side as well and pulling her closer to him.

"This means—" She paused long enough that he tickled her. When he stopped and she caught her breath, she continued. "We'll have to find ways to play by ourselves. Our crew, our team, our... I don't know. What do we call them?"

He shook his head in answer.

She scrunched her nose. "Well, whatever term we use to identify them—they have abandoned their life of frivolity and left us behind. In our time of need."

"Our time of need?"

Violet nodded fervently. Yes, their time of need, if you considered being spoiled and bored and time of need—then certainly.

"So, we'll go to dinner just the two of us," he suggested. "It'll be hard, I know, to spend so much time together, but we'll have to persevere." He sounded aghast, but she knew the sound of his teasing.

Jack lifted himself on one elbow and loomed over her. She wasn't all that small for a woman, but Jack was a beast of a man. He was taller than anyone she'd ever met, with broad shoulders, large biceps and a square jawline that she adored. She ran her fingers over his stubble, enjoying the prickling feeling against her fingertips.

"I suppose I could survive an evening with just you," she mused idly. "We might have to find new friends if that doesn't work. I don't think Kate will leave the country until she can move without sicking up."

"She does seem to be the most ill expectant mother I have ever encountered," Jack told Violet, trailing his finger down her nose. "It quite turns one off of the whole idea of children."

"She said her mother was the same. Grandmother as

well. It's terrifying to see," Violet said frankly. "Mostly because I worry about myself."

Jack's snort of laughter was just the way to finish waking up. She'd dreamed the night before of everyone having babies and immediately dumped her thoughts on him. She nestled against him. "There is something utterly luxurious about waking when we choose and laying about like this. I don't think Victor and Kate have experienced this kind of luxury since Kate was expecting the twins."

"Given that she was expecting before they married, and she's so sick while expectant," Jack pointed out, "they may well have never enjoyed these quiet moments."

He trailed his finger across Vi's cheekbones as if experiencing her face for the first time. At times, when he looked at her, she felt as though she might well be the loveliest woman to ever live, but she knew that though lively and pretty enough, her features weren't noteworthy.

"So, what are we going to do then?" he asked as he brushed a lock of her bobbed hair out of her face. "Drum up our old friends and beg them to come out with us? Adventure alone? Just stay in bed until Victor and Denny's children are old enough that their parents will play full-time again?"

Vi flopped onto her back. "I suspect that I could stand to go dancing with you alone. Or dive into one of those scavenger hunts. Or perhaps we should get a yacht—"

"If we get a yacht," he told her flatly, "we're getting a man to sail it. I have no desire to stay up all night when necessary."

"You," she told him with a wicked twist to her mouth,

"are spoilt. Getting a man—" she scoffed, "—saying it like you're getting a pair of shoes."

"This is what comes from marrying an earl's daughter. I really should have considered that vicar's daughter from my hometown before allowing you to corrupt me."

Vi gasped but couldn't hold in the laughter. When she quieted, she told him, "Speaking of being spoilt, I think I'll get some new dresses for going out. I'll need to attract other men because who wants to dance with just one man? I need to—" She couldn't finish her comment because he was too quick to silence her.

JACK HAD an appointment for lunch with his father, so he was gone by the time Violet had dressed. After lingering in bed, she lingered in the bath, and then over her cosmetics, dressing, and playing with her dogs. She made her way to Beatrice's office, but her one-time maid had a visitor, so Violet faded away before she could bother them.

"I am bored," she told her dogs, Rouge and Holmes, as she walked back to the parlor. Holmes put his paw on her leg to beg for some love. She complied while she considered working on her book. Only, Victor was too far away at his country home to collaborate easily with and she'd already sent him several chapters to respond to. She really should wait for his notes and his chapters. Her mouth screwed up as she considered writing on her own, but it was simply more fun with her brother.

She frowned at the wall in the library, considered re-reading her favorite Edgar Rice Burroughs novels and the idea filled her with exhaustion. She decided instead to call for a black cab, but once inside, she sat staring forward with a frown long enough for the fellow to lift his brows and ask, "You want to go somewhere or not?"

Violet paused too long and then said, "Ah, oh. Why not Harrod's?"

His scoff at her question had her waving him on and wishing she hadn't been dim enough to phrase it as a question.

When she arrived, she made a reservation for tea and then wandered through the store. She found beautiful teddy bears in a soft tan and a soft cream for her twin nieces, it didn't matter that it had just been Christmas. Violet bought the bears for the girls and then went to find something for Victor that would cheer him while Kate was ill. Truthfully, Violet felt only helplessness when it came to her sister-in-law. Poor Kate was ill incessantly while expecting and what could you do for her? Nothing but ginger candies and peppermints.

Violet wandered until she came across the tearoom, making purchases more out of boredom than anything else.

"Perhaps," she mused aloud despite being alone, "I shouldn't have let Beatrice take over the business side of my life." Vi didn't want to go back to working more closely with her business interests, but she truly was just so bored.

A woman with narrowed eyes and round spectacles glanced at Violet, mouth pursed sourly. Violet tried a winning grin, but it didn't help. Instead she winked and turned back to the tearoom, asking if there was room for her yet. It was still before the time they had given her, but she was bored with shopping as well.

The maitre'd looked her over. It had been someone else who had put her on the list before. Vi was wearing a nice enough dress to pass, but having tea in a place like Harrod's was an event, and she was clearly only dropping by. Her grey dress with layers of scalloped edges and embroidery along the wrists was, however, fabulous. But, perhaps, not fabulous enough.

He paused and then asked, "Name?"

"Violet Wakefield," she replied cheerily enough and then heard another voice repeat her name.

"Violet? Vi! Oh my heavens, I thought that was you. Whatever are you doing here alone? I was just talking about us having been school chums."

"Phoebe Rees? Is it really you?" Violet laughed. "Shopping out of boredom," Violet answered, kissing the air next to the girl's face.

"Oh," Phoebe said happily. "How long has it been? I feel like I was much smaller the last time we were together."

Violet laughed again but she glanced down anxiously. Phoebe was also expecting and Vi hid her immediate disappointment. Coming across an old friend had the feel of fate, but it seemed her conversation with Jack that morning had not announced to the world what she needed, for the world had not provided the womanly friend she'd envisioned – one ready for late nights and later mornings, for clubs and dining and frivolity. If she was going to be friends with an expectant woman, it might as well be Lila. She might be lazy and always sarcastic and—at the moment—too round and tired to go dancing, but even on her worst of days, Lila was the best of friends.

"Come!" Phoebe declared. "Tea with us! Oh do get another chair, my good man! My sister is here," she continued to Violet. "And my mother-in-law," Phoebe's nose wrinkled, but she grinned again. "I fear too many sisters-in-law and cousins-in-law. Did you know that I married Harold? Of course you did. You called me Rees. So funny to change names isn't it? What's yours again?"

"Wakefield." Violet considered declining, but the man had already sent for another chair.

Phoebe laughed merrily and then pulled Violet across the floor with her to the table where tiered plates were stacked high with bite-sized treats. Violet let herself be drawn more out of boredom than a desire to reconnect. Phoebe had been one of the girls at Violet's school and they'd been friendly enough. The kind of acquaintance who enjoyed a good catch-up and never wrote during the holidays.

"Is this your first?" Violet asked Phoebe under her breath as they approached the table.

"Second," Phoebe said with a grin. "My first was a daughter, alas. Harold and I have a bargain that once we have two sons, we're finished."

"Finished?"

"No more children. Little Alice is a darling, of course. But I should like to be done with children."

Phoebe stopped whispering and grinned at Violet before announcing to the table, "Look who it is! Violet Carlyle. Wakefield now."

An old woman looked up and scowled at Violet before glancing her over. "Lady Violet?"

"I fear so." Violet smiled around the group, knowing that it was a bit untoward that she was jumping into what was clearly a family party, but boredom very rarely was alleviated with manners. "Through my father, I'm afraid."

"Join us." The woman's head tilted slightly, and Violet guessed this wasn't the mother-in-law but grandmother or great aunt. Someone of the generation beyond. Her hands were spotted with age, her glasses were held onto her face with pearls, and the jewelry was nearly as thick on Mrs. Stevens as Violet preferred to wear. She had, however, been too bored that morning to layer on the jewels. "I knew your grandmother," the old woman said.

"I'm afraid I did not," Violet replied, maintaining a cheery polite tone even though it was not how she preferred to start a conversation.

"She was a snob and uppity."

Violet blinked as the rest of the woman's party turned towards Violet in horror. This old woman was painfully direct. Violet wasn't certain if that was going to be good or bad, so she opted for sarcasm. "I would assume so given my father."

"Look at them," the old woman said, gesturing to her family. "They look like a bunch of suffocating fish, gaping at an old woman for telling the truth." The woman's mouth turned up at that and she said in her crackling voice, "I, too, am a snob and uppity. Always have been."

"I believe," Violet told her as though confessing but with a twist of her lips, "that I can only claim to be uppity."

"Yes, well, your mother wasn't really one of us, was she? You're the one who was born to Lady Penelope."

"Happily," Violet said with enough of an edge that the old woman nodded. That had been too direct and entirely unwanted. Violet might only have the merest of wisps of memories of her mother, but they were precious to her, and she'd be damned before she'd let some uppity, snobbish, and rude old woman color those.

"Indeed. She was uppity too, and I liked her more than I liked your grandmother."

Violet shook her head, uncertain how to take that, but the building grudge against the woman was instantly forgiven. Phoebe saved her from needing to respond.

"Allow me to introduce you to Mrs. Macie Stevens," Phoebe said. "Harold's great aunt."

"Delighted," Violet replied. Of all the people at the table only Mrs. Stevens met Violet's gaze with the same wicked smirk Violet herself was known for. It seemed perhaps that Violet's wish had been heard after all, though she didn't expect the woman to be a peer with her grandmother rather than herself.

CHAPTER 2

*V*iolet ordered a cup of tea and then placed a small pot of custard topped with chocolate curls on her plate. She took a single petit-four as Mrs. Stevens asked, "Tell me, Violet. What do you do with yourself during the days?"

"Nothing much," Violet admitted. "I fear I'm spoiled as earl's daughters often are."

Mrs. Stevens grinned. "That's not what I hear."

Violet knew immediately of what she was speaking of, of course. "I fear the tales of my exploits are over told."

"Are they?" Mrs. Stevens mouth twisted and she said, "Did you know I am quite fond of Miss Emily Allen. I know all about you and Jack Wakefield. I did ask her for news recently after... certain events."

Violet snorted. "Those are not tales for an afternoon tea, I'm afraid. When you add in that Miss Allen is not my biggest fan, I fear what tales of horror you've been told."

"Then you shall have to come to my house party and tell me all about it then."

"A house party?" Phoebe asked, frowning.

"Oh Aunt Stevens, surely not," one of the older women said. "It's a little—"

Whatever the woman was going to say was cut off by Mrs. Stevens firmly stating, "A house party. Two weekends from now. I'll send you my card. Do come."

The last bit was phrased as an order and Violet considered rebellion, and then she reconsidered and decided to go, more out of a desire to make Jack come with her rather than on another one of Ham's cases. Jack had been shot on the last one and Violet didn't feel like she was made of the same material as women who sent their men into danger time after time.

Violet nodded. "That does sound interesting."

It sounded boring and Jack would see through her attempt, but she didn't care in the least. He could see through it and deal with the effects of his being shot. He'd made that choice for both of them. He had pushed her into terror at losing him, gratitude at his breath, and now she was bearing the fury of nearly losing him to his choice. If she had to drag him to some random house party to keep him from another case, she'd do it.

Mrs. Stevens caught Violet's lie and was amused at it. Violet could guess that this woman, with all her age, was someone who had experienced all Vi was currently struggling with and probably all the burdens she had yet to bear. The house party might not be a complete failure then, as observing Mrs. Stevens with a household of guests could prove entertaining.

Violet listened to the women of the Rees family as they cast each other pointed gibes and smiled in the face of meanness while she barely held back, shaking her head at the pettiness.

"What will you call your next daughter?" one of the other younger women asked Phoebe. "You're carrying as though it's another girl. Won't that be nice to have two little angels?"

Violet winched for Phoebe at the gibe and at the term angel said with barely disguised sarcasm. That was what Lila and Denny used for their baby but that child was wanted. Phoebe had made it clear she had no desire for another girl.

Phoebe had paled at the idea but she tried to cover for it. "Perhaps we'll call her Macie." Phoebe turned to Mrs. Stevens and asked, "Would you like that?"

"My fortune is already accounted for, girl. Naming your babe after me won't get her something when I die." With a pause, Mrs. Stevens face softened and she offered, "I think you look as though you could be carrying a boy. What does Delilah know about carrying children?"

The woman who had spoken so meanly to Phoebe flinched and then paled herself, but she also had a haunted look that went beyond being called out. It seemed that Delilah was not as blessed as Phoebe.

Was she unable to conceive? Violet cast Mrs. Stevens a dark look. Why would anyone taunt a woman about being unable to carry a child? Vi was already regretting accepting the house party invitation. Not even Violet's unliked stepmother would make such a taunt, and Lady

Eleanor was as snobbish and uppity as a woman in her position could be.

The possibility might explain Delilah's cruelty toward Phoebe. It must be hard for Delilah to want a child and not be blessed while Phoebe might be carrying a daughter she did not want.

"You're leaving the money to Peter, are you not?" Delilah asked, blinking away a tear. "He's a good nephew."

"Is this what it was like for your aunt?" Mrs. Stevens asked Violet. "Everyone squabbling over her money before one of you killed her?"

"Yes," Violet said flatly, entirely unamused. She set aside her custard pot and placed her hands in her lap to hide the fists.

"Oh Aunt Stevens," one of the other older women said. Violet had already forgotten her name, but she liked the sound of the woman's disgust.

"Thank you for the tea." She placed her napkin next to her plate and advised, "If I were you, I'd leave all your money to charity and spend your final days on a warm island."

"That is good advice," Mrs. Stevens replied quietly with a dark look at her children. "I'll consider it."

"Mmm," Violet said, not wanting to agree or disagree. She wanted to pour her tea on the lap of the woman who callously referenced the murder of Violet's aunt.

"Good advice indeed." Mrs. Steven's mouth was as sour as ever and her condemning look extended to everyone present at the table. "Your aunt should have followed it."

Grief stabbed Violet as she rose. "It was a pleasure to

see you again, Phoebe," she said, having to strain for politeness. "Thank you for allowing me to join your tea."

Violet nodded to everyone and then fled the tea. It had been delicious but not worth the emotional turmoil. If she were going to observe the fighting of a family, Violet preferred it to be one where she could understand the undercurrents and pettiness behind the gibes. Having to weave the pieces together and understand how cruel they were being to each other, it was more than Violet wanted to handle. Especially when the undercurrent felt too much like Violet's great aunt's death. It was a loss that Violet would never shake. Having it tossed into the conversation so casually hadn't helped.

She left the tearoom listless. Violet paused as she realized that she was feeling blue. Perhaps that was why she didn't want to write. She shook her head. Of course it was. It was why she didn't want to write, why she was so angry with Jack, and why nothing sounded fun.

She wasn't going to decline back into those days again if she could help it in the least. Vi wasn't arrogant enough to believe it was utterly in her control, but if nothing else, she could fight it. She walked towards the doors of Harrod's, considered the rain, and frowned. The grey days matched what was happening inside of her heart.

She needed to move so she could flush away as much of the growing despair with exercise as she could, one remedy she'd had luck with in the past, but she had no desire to do so in the rain.

"It's a day for either strolling in the rain and enjoying it," the doorman said, "or sending for a black cab."

Violet started to tell the man to send for a black cab

and then paused. "No. Have the packages sent to my home, will you?" She handed him her card and then told him. "Now an umbrella and I think I'll do just as you suggested."

Violet purchased a large black umbrella and tipped the man generously, laughing at the look on his face as she stepped into the street and tilted the umbrella over her head. As she left Harrod's, Vi saw Mrs. Stevens through the window. The old woman lifted a brow disagreeably. Out of sheer madness, Vi spun in a circle, curtsied, and then noticed a puddle in front of her. She shrugged and jumped into the puddle, remembering how much she liked doing so as a child.

"Oh," Violet said in dismay. "That is uncomfortable."

Her toes squelched in her shoes.

"You don't have the right shoes, lady." A well-dressed boy loitering nearby was watching her in amusement.

Violet glanced at him and then at her soaked shoes. "Too right you are, young sir."

"You've gotta at least have good boots." He rubbed his coat sleeve along his nose and sniffed deeply.

"What are you doing here? Don't you have school?"

"Who's got time for school?" he countered.

"Given your fine jacket, my good lad, I suspect your mother thinks you've time for school."

He grinned at her. "Don't tell her, will you?"

Vi lifted a brow and he shrugged lightly as though he were prepared for either outcome.

"So," he said, stepping closer, "have you gone mad?"

"Perhaps a little," Violet admitted, "I'm struggling to be happy."

He eyed her again, frowning deeply. "What for?

You've got a fancy dress. Came out of the fancy store. You're grown up. You can probably do whatever you want."

Violet leaned against the wall, tilting her umbrella over both of their heads. "You would think so, wouldn't you? If you could buy anything, what would it be?"

"A dog," he said immediately. "One that likes to run and plays fetch and has a big happy face."

"Does your mother say no?"

He frowned and shook his head. "My father says I'm not responsible enough."

Violet's mouth twisted with sympathy. "Are you? Dogs are quite a lot of trouble, you know. I have two and servants to help me and yet I still end up running the dogs to the garden, rubbing their bellies when they don't feel well, and I have been messed on more than once."

"I wouldn't mind that so much," he told her seriously and Violet was certain it was true.

"Then you should ask your father what you need to do to get a dog." He scowled at her darkly and she understood. "Oh ho. You have."

"He said I had to earn the money to get a dog."

Violet lifted her brows. "Is this how you're doing it?" Her tone had him blushing. "Loitering outside of tea shops?"

"I help the old ladies across the street and am charming and sweet for tips. How else am I supposed to do it? I'm no good at shining shoes."

"What do you think your father will do when he discovers that you've left school to earn money for a dog?"

The boy blushed more deeply.

"Do you know," Violet told him thoughtfully, "I have quite the need of a good dog walker."

He rubbed his arm over his nose again and then scratched his head under his cap, eyeing her as if expecting a trick. "I think I need to go to school before Father realizes."

"Mmm," Violet agreed. "Your troubles are more easily solved than mine, I fear."

"Being happy isn't so hard," the boy told her. "You just do what you want to do."

"I wish it really were so easy."

The boy pshawed. Violet handed him her card. "My dogs are spoiled and prefer the warmth of home. I'll be needing you to teach them to fetch as well."

"You meant it about the dog-walking? You weren't putting me on?"

"No, I was not putting you on."

He took the card, eyes bright.

"It won't be all fun and games," Violet told him flatly. "I'm not going to help you sidestep your father. Just give you a job. You will still be expected to attend school."

He was nodding happily, no doubt dreaming of playing with the dogs in the garden and giving them treats to learn tricks.

"I mean it," Violet warned. "I'll come up with horrible errands beyond playing with my dogs."

"I'll do them," he said eagerly.

Violet shook her head at him and then glanced down at her shoes.

"You know what makes me happy and helped me out," he said in a tone of a person older than his years, which she put at about ten. "What makes you happy?"

"My family. My husband. Helping people."

"So, do those things, lady."

"I do try, but they aren't always possible." She sighed and finally confessed what was truly bothering her. "I'm angry at my husband for getting hurt." The boy's scoff was echoed by Violet's. "I know it isn't reasonable. But a part of me thinks that it is reasonable. He was doing a dangerous job that he didn't have to do and now I'm afraid he could be hurt again and he's wrapped up in all the happiness I've been able to scrape together."

The boy pshawed once again.

Violet, however, ignored the boy. She added, "I've come to depend on him being there, but he did something dangerous and was hurt." Saying it aloud made it sound even more unreasonable. "I could lose him."

"Was it something that had to be done by somebody?" the boy asked, clearly on Jack's side. Oh men! Sticking together with little regard to the importance their continued living provided to those who loved them.

Violet sighed as she nodded. "Yes, it was quite necessary."

The boy lifted a brow nearly as sardonic as one that Jack could give.

Vi glanced out at the rain and the dirty street and then down at her muddy feet, then at the boy she'd just spilled her fears to. "Oy, I've gone mad."

He laughed at her, which made her grin. She held out her hand, "Violet Wakefield."

"Leo Marshall." He shook her hand firmly, giving her arm two solid pumps.

"What do you do when you aren't sad?" Leo asked.

"Write. Go to clubs. Play, I suppose. I used to run my business, but I gave it over to my friend."

"Why'd you do that?"

Violet frowned deeply as she replied, "I wanted her to be happy, and she does it better."

"My mother says idle hands are a devil's workshop."

"I think I would like her," Violet told him. The rain was picking up, and as much as she was enjoying the conversation, oddly enough, she wasn't going to let the boy stand out all day in the rain. "Get to school," she told him sternly, but she winked at him.

He nodded and ran off, but he cast a wink back at her that told Violet he wasn't going to obey.

It wasn't her problem, Vi thought, though if he were to work for her, it might become so. She turned back towards her house. It really was too far to walk and she was awkwardly wet. Violet hailed a black cab for herself and took a seat in the back, giving the man her address.

"Do you know what my problem is?" Violet asked the cabbie, staring out the window as the streets of London passed her by.

"You're batty." He'd eyed her muddy shoes as she'd climbed in.

"I think so, yes," Violet agreed. She laughed low without humor and said, "I really am the most spoilt woman I have ever known."

CHAPTER 3

*V*iolet faced her house, glanced down at her sodden shoes and muddy stockings, and knew with utter certainty that she'd never escape without having to explain herself. She walked up the steps, grateful at least that she'd worn a good coat. She supposed an idle fancy would explain leaping into a puddle, but she knew what was happening with her was more than that.

She found Jack inside the parlor, reading the newspaper with a bourbon in his hand and she stared at him for a long minute before she confessed, "I'm angry with you."

"I've noticed." Those penetrating eyes of his passed her over, taking in her sodden feet and the umbrella and he tossed the newspaper aside before he continued. "What are we going to do about it?"

"I'm rather selfish of your life, you know."

He set down his bourbon and slowly rose as she

crossed to take the chair next to him. Rather than sitting back down, he settled onto the ottoman and pulled her wet foot into his lap, removing her shoe and rolling her stockings down and off.

"I like that you're selfish of my life."

Violet hated that her eyes were filling with tears. "I would say I can't lose you, but I can. Can't I? Nothing prevents it from happening. What more can a slew of murders in our lives teach us but that life is fragile and easily stolen."

"It teaches us to cherish the moment," Jack added.

"The fact that I almost did lose you is making me feel both like a spoiled brat since I know you were needed and like a wilting flower for being so weak."

Jack rubbed her feet and his eyes were as full of emotion as hers. "I'm afraid loss is rather a part of life and we can't live in fear of it, can we?"

"No," Violet agreed, leaning back. "I don't want to live like that either. I don't want to be a wilting, spoilt flower or sucked into the blues."

Jack let his hands grasp her ankles and leaned forward to place a kiss on her forehead. "You are neither wilting nor spoilt and your fight against the blues is inspiring. You're witty and fun and you give yourself fully to the people you love, and you hand over parts of yourself far too generously."

Violet laughed and then told him of the boy outside of Harrod's and of Mrs. Stevens.

"She sounds like an odd woman."

When she told him of the reference to Aunt Agatha, his jaw flexed in anger and he said, "I was invited to a scavenger hunt for Saturday. It starts at midnight. At the same time, these fools were mentioning your murdered aunt to you casually over tea? As though what happened to her were some sort of joke? Casually discussing her murder with someone who loved her while nibbling biscuits?"

Violet bit her bottom lip to hide the rush of emotion that hit her whenever they discussed the death of her aunt. Aunt Agatha was the woman who had raised Violet and her twin. There was nothing about her death that was casual for Violet. Losing a good parent effected someone for the whole of their lives. Having someone you adored stolen from you was beyond devastating.

"Oh," Violet said, "Did you know that Miss Allen has been discussing us with this woman?"

"How could I know that?"

"Why would she?" Vi demanded. Emily Allen had been engaged to be married to Jack at one point. She'd thrown him over and come to regret her decision, but Violet and Jack had already found each other. "She does have a life of her own beyond us."

Jack's expression said he wasn't quite sure how to answer.

"Well," Violet said, pausing when she heard a bit of a ruckus at the door. They'd let the fellows who watched their house go since there hadn't been an attempt on the house since they'd been plagued by a prankster. They hadn't, however, lost their awareness of the noises and surroundings.

Jack set Violet's feet back on the floor and rose, leaning forward to look at the door. There was no knock but the sound of rustling occurred again.

"Please no mice," Violet muttered, following Jack as

they approached the door. "I'll never get past the mice, I don't think."

A moment later a letter was shoved through the slot. Violet frowned. It was far past the time when the postman should arrive. Jack leaned down to pick up the letter and then opened the door. They could see an auto pulling away, but whoever had just shoved that letter through the slot must have flown down the stairs and into the waiting auto.

Jack started to close the door, but Violet placed a hand on his arm. The deliverer of the letter had placed a brick in front of the gate to prop it open, no doubt to make a hasty escape. Vi ran down the steps in her bare feet and lifted the brick. It wasn't from her house and she glanced about before setting it next to the gate and shutting it. Had the letter-deliverer brought the brick? Why did anyone want to deliver a note anonymously?

She turned to Jack, whose expression was baffled as he looked at her toes. "I'm calling for coffee for those poor cold feet of yours."

Violet laughed. Jack nudged her towards the stairs. "New stockings, Vi. You're going to catch your death."

"What about the letter?"

Jack shook his head. "I'll send for coffee and read it. It's probably an invitation to a Sunday meeting. Nothing to worry about."

Vi lifted her brow at that malarkey. She didn't have Jack's nearly all-seeing gaze, but she knew him better than that and the world better than that, too. He was worried about the contents of the letter, probably especially after her hijinks of the day. He wanted to see what it was, given the odd way it was delivered, and given how she had been behaving, he wanted to protect her.

Violet shrugged and ran up the stairs. She took one look at herself in the mirror and decided Jack might have a point. Her feet were dirty from the muddy water and the barefoot trip outside. Her dress was splashed with mud with the nonsense of jumping in that puddle. Her hair was wind-blown and messy and the kohl about her eyes had smudged.

"Oh Vi," she told herself. She could shove on stockings and a clean dress and race back down to learn the contents of the letter, but she was still worn around the edges from the day and her feet were cold. Instead, she drew a hot bath. A dip into the hot, scented water and a quick scrub of her face left her red-cheeked, but not quite the drowned rat she had been. She kicked her messed dress to the side and opened her closet door, considering a dress or a kimono.

It was their cook's night off, so they had intended to go out to dinner, but Violet threw that idea to the wind when she slid on warm knit socks and a pair of red silk pajamas. Her pajamas were embroidered with dragons in gold thread at both the ankles and wrists. She topped it with her favorite red and gold kimono and then threw herself on the bed.

The coffee wouldn't be ready yet and she quite enjoyed luxuriously relaxing on the bed just before dinner. She should dress for dinner, but she was far more inclined to suggest to Jack that they eat in their bedroom, turn on the wireless, and enjoy an evening by the fire rather than out.

She hadn't forgotten the letter, but she was unwilling

to let its presence dictate her actions. Much better to relax for a time and let the blues grow distant and let Jack puzzle it out first.

Jack appeared in the doorway and his head tilted at her pajamas. "It's Cook's night out."

"Yes." She turned over, pushing up on her hands so she was half-sitting, half-reclined.

"Shall I go for Indian food?" he asked.

She waited. He'd come to her, which meant there was something in the letter he would rather she not know, but he knew she wasn't going to stand for him wrapping her in wool as he clearly wanted. It took only a look for that understanding to pass between them.

He closed his eyes. "It was a claim of murder."

Vi paused, shocked. "And? They want us to investigate? Rather than the professionals?"

"You, actually," Jack corrected. "Not me. If some nameless fellow thinks they're going to haul you into a murder investigation alone, they just might incite a second murder."

Violet laughed. "Are you offended they asked for me?" She was relieved that they hadn't requested Jack.

He shook his head with a frown.

"Who was murdered?" she asked.

"A man named Olly Rees."

"What?" Violet gasped. "Rees?"

"Yes, I noted the coincidence, too. The same day you meet an old friend who has married into the Rees family you also receive a letter about the possible murder of a man bearing the same name."

"It wasn't signed, was it?" Violet asked, holding out her hand and Jack handed the letter over.

. . .

DEAR LADY VIOLET,

I turn to you with great horror and hope that the tales of your kindness have not been exaggerated. It has become clearer and clearer to me over the last days that a terrible crime has occurred. Olly Rees died recently. He was quite old, however, he was also quite mobile and strong. His sudden death was attributed to age by all involved, but I cannot believe the same.

IT IS my opinion that Olly was murdered. I have heard tales of your cleverness and ability to sleuth out the truth. Won't you help us? Help him? He was a good fellow who deserved better than he received. Won't you prevent a murderer from getting away with their crime and set this family to rights?

SIGNED,

A Concerned Family Member

JACK SAT DOWN NEXT to her, taking the letter and reading it over again.

"You don't believe this is a coincidence," she said to him, her stomach sinking, "and I don't either. Mrs. Stevens did say she was going to invite me to a house party. It was a rather sudden declaration. Maybe this is why."

Jack shook his head. "I'd hate to put my foot down, darling—"

Violet choked on the waterfall of sarcasm that wanted to pour from her mouth. He was the one who'd been shot. Though, she had to admit she'd been in a few near-misses herself. Instead, she looked at him, remembered how very much she loved him and said, "You won't have to, of course."

The relaxing of his stiffness was just what she wanted to see. She placed her hand over his and then waited until he turned to her.

"Why would we go?" he asked. "An imagined crime and a waste of our time."

Violet considered. "Thinking back, I suspect that Mrs. Stevens might also believe that this Olly was murdered. She said she'd asked Miss Allen about us. Why would any woman who didn't know us do so?"

"Odd that you ran into them at the tea shop," Jack agreed. "Odd that the old woman knew who you were and had already inquired after you."

"Odd, yes. But what if we were going to get this letter regardless? What if she was pursuing information about us—" She grinned and amended it to, "me—regardless?"

"Or," Jack guessed, "what if there is more than one person who suspected murder? What if your friend was thinking it and then saw you at the tea shop and jumped at the opportunity to speak with you? At the same time, Mrs. Stevens was suspecting foul play and asked her friend, Miss Allen, about who might be able to help her?"

"I think the question is whether we also believe that the man was murdered."

Jack laid back, pulling her down beside him so they

were both facing the ceiling. "I don't know about that and I don't know about whether we should allow ourselves to be pulled in."

Playing the devil's advocate, Violet asked. "If we refuse the invitation and there was a murder, will we be haunted by not doing something?"

They both knew they would be though neither of them admitted it.

"But can we allow ourselves to be pulled into any random claim of murder when someone doesn't want to believe their relative shouldn't be dead?"

Violet didn't disagree and she didn't have any real fondness for her school chum, Phoebe, and no connection to the rest of the family. But she did think she might end up being haunted if there were reason to believe that he was murdered and the chance to discover what happened had passed.

Vi turned onto her side and snuggled closer to Jack. "I think we should find out what we can about Olly Rees and then decide."

Jack considered this and Violet could see the need in his gaze to avoid being trapped again, but he nodded. "You have too bright of an imagination, darling. I can see you imagining the old man being killed and the family laughing in the background."

Violet laughed, but he was right. "The young heroine wishing to help, yet unable to discover how and why and so denied the chance to proceed. Haunted for the rest of her life."

"Her life?"

Violet rolled her eyes at him.

He snorted. "Fine then, her life. They asked only for

you. You saw them at the tea. One of the women there must have been the one who asked for your help."

Violet pressed a kiss on his chin and suggested that an omelet, bread, coffee and cheese were worth staying in on a such a rainy day. "Since a man would never ask a woman for help."

"I suppose we can look into it," Jack said kindly.

Violet suppressed a triumphant grin.

"And then tomorrow we hunt down your father."

Vi scrunched her nose.

"If this Mrs. Stevens knew your mother and grandmother, she knows your father. He may well know more about Olly Rees or know someone who knew him."

"Fine," Violet said, huffing and then followed him to the kitchens. The house was mostly empty with it being the servants' half-day. There was a daily maid to answer the door and make coffee, but the rest of the live-in servants were out. Violet and Jack made themselves a meal by grabbing what looked good from the kitchens and taking it up to their bedroom for a picnic by the fire.

CHAPTER 4

*V*i had to admit she struggled with her feelings for her father. She both loved him and found him disappointing. As a father, he'd been distant to non-existent in her life. But he'd also handed her and Victor to their aunt. Aunt Agatha was able to cut through their grief for their mother and help them be children again. It was an act of ineffable love, but it also hurt to realize that he'd let go after that. Regardless, he was her father and she knew he cared.

"Father," Violet said, leaning down to kiss his cheek and then sitting in the chair that Jack pulled out for her. "How are you?"

She listened as he discussed her brother, Geoffrey, her stepmother, and his cronies. When the waiter appeared, she ordered a Bee's Knees, feeling like a little honey might make the sourness of discussing potential murder a little easier.

Once the waiter left, her fathered huffed. "What's wrong?"

Violet paused, realizing her heart was warmed by his question. He was ready to help. "Jack and I have been drawn into an oddness and we were wondering if you could give us some insight."

"Oddness?" Father asked.

"Violet was drawn in," Jack told her father with a laugh. "She was asked to help with a recent death that someone thinks may have been murder."

"Someone or some she? Of course it must be a woman, but Vi does have a reputation for cleverness." Her father smiled and then he grew serious before he asked, "Was it for Olly Rees?"

Violet and Jack both turned to him, mouths dropped as they stared. "How did you know?"

"I don't care if that man was in his eighties," Father said without answering. "He was as strong as a horse and his father lived to a hundred. The last time I saw him, we were hunting, and I couldn't keep up with the codger. He was sprightly, completely mentally aware, and as savvy as he was in his twenties, if I had to guess."

"Was he really?" Violet asked. "Why was it determined to not be murder then?"

"Any reasonable police officer," Jack said, "would have looked at the death of a man in his eighties and assumed it was age if there were no overt signs of murder. Why wouldn't it be? I assume he wasn't stabbed or shot."

"No, of course not," the earl replied. He sighed deeply, the most emotion he'd shown about the death of this supposed friend. "Perhaps it was necessary to know him and see him moving about. I'd bet my last pound he was murdered or something else untoward happened. A terrible accident, perhaps, but why would anyone cover that up?"

When the waiter returned, they discussed the weather until the drinks were set before them, so their conversation would remain private, but Violet was turning over the new information in her mind. Having more than simply a name, getting pieces that put together Olly Rees as a living person made the possibility of his murder so much worse.

She could so easily imagine some older gent out-walking her father while hunting partridges or whatever her father hunted. It wasn't a sport that Violet had any desire to delve into.

"Why would anyone kill your friend?" Violet asked after the waiter left. She took a healthy sip of her drink, which had been mixed perfectly, but honey still wasn't enough to sooth the bitter taste that came from speaking of murder—especially with her father who left her on edge and a bit sour anyway.

"I don't know," the earl replied. "He was well enough off, but I don't imagine the money—even before death duties—it was not enough to murder over. His two sons are the likely inheritors, possibly with a small amount for each of his grandchildren."

"Are they in need, do you think?" Jack asked. "The money will always be the first motive for a rich fellow like this man."

"I believe they are both quite fine financially. Unless there was some secret, desperate need, he was a good man and a good father. I can't imagine either of his sons hurting him for a small increase." He let the thought trail off.

Violet bit down on her bottom lip. "Meredith killed Aunt Agatha for less reason than that."

Her father reached out and took her hand. "Meredith wasn't normal, Vi."

She stared at her cocktail, hiding her rush of fury. "No one who is normal kills another person. Meredith knew she wasn't going to inherit a fortune and she killed for barely anything."

The earl sighed. "Meredith killed to escape her untenable life and stole something from you that can't be replaced. Vi—"

Violet frowned, withdrawing her hand from his, not wanting to hear what he would say. The platitudes never helped.

He was bothered by the way she yanked her hand back. She could see it in him. The little crumbs of affection he sent her way were never enough to satisfy her need for a father, so they just hurt more.

"There isn't an apology for Aunt Agatha being killed. Nothing makes it better. I don't understand. It doesn't matter how many people I see murdered by those in their lives who are supposed to love them—I don't understand it. I would never, ever kill anyone for money or for any other reason. What possible reason could someone have to kill your friend? Because I don't understand. No matter how many times I see it, I can't understand. Especially some kindly old man."

The earl looked to Jack as if he could translate why Violet was so upset and then carefully asked her, "Why are you so upset? You didn't know him, Vi."

Violet stared. "Does it not matter because I couldn't see the effect this has on people who knew and loved him? I might not have known him, but it doesn't have to be only the death of a friend to affect me. It ruins whatever joy I can scrape together to think of someone grieving a loss, especially one that needn't have happened. You are here, you're alive. Olly isn't. Someone took that from him and they stole from those who loved him all the time that they might have had together."

Violet rose and walked away from the table, knowing that she had lost control of her emotions. She heard Jack say, "Some old woman asked Violet callously about Agatha yesterday. Vi is still—" Jack trailed off and her father's reply was too low to hear. Violet kept walking. It was like an unholy rage was rushing through her, prickling her veins from inside of her body, and she was furious all over again about losing Aunt Agatha let alone every death that had come thereafter.

The truth was—if she were being selfish and unkind —how this man's death brought up the murder of the woman who raised Violet. There just wasn't an easy way to get over that. You didn't forget that the woman who you adored and looked up to over the course of your life was stabbed in her office by someone she loved.

Violet headed towards the ladies' room to cool down. She approached the mirror, turned on the cold water and let it run over her wrists. The prickling behind her skin wasn't lessening and Violet closed her eyes, breathing in slowly and letting it out even slower. Slow breaths, counting, cold water, and too long of a time and Violet was almost afraid she wouldn't be able to cool down.

She stared at herself in the mirror, ignoring the attendant. Someone had murdered Olly Rees just as Meredith had murdered Violet's aunt. Possibly. Had that person possibly poisoned his after-dinner drink? Put arsenic in his sweets? Held a pillow over his face? When she imagined the amorphous old man the vision of him faded into a version of her aunt. The limbs twitching under the pillow were Aunt Agatha's and even though Agatha was already dead, Violet was nauseated at the image. She shuddered and closed her eyes again. She didn't want to think these things. She wished she could be one of those bright young things who only thought about clothes, lovers, and parties.

Finally, the rage started to flee. She deliberately considered the dress she had bought earlier. It wasn't anything to keep in her mind, but whatever it took to refocus her mind. It took too long to cool down and by the time she left the ladies' room, her father was waiting in the hall.

"I was worried."

"I'm fine," she lied blatantly. His gaze didn't sharpen at all, and she realized he had no idea what was going through her mind.

"It's not fine, Vi. Neither what happened to Agatha nor perhaps what happened to Olly."

Violet shook her head. She had just calmed down. "I don't want to talk about it."

"Olly wasn't incredibly wealthy," her father said, taking on a business tone, "but he did have a nice little country house with an excellent wood nearby, some money in savings, and a few collectibles that would have been worth killing over."

"What do you mean?"

"I mean he's from an old enough family that it's possible they're passing around priceless heirlooms. To so many of our kind, people are handing down art that was bought by the grandmother and painted by a Renaissance master."

Violet's brows lifted and she considered. It felt possible. After all, she'd inherited art and jewelry. When she saw some of the art, she didn't think of the painter even if it was one of the ancient masters. Vi thought of looking at it in Aunt Agatha's bedroom and the memory of days with her aunt. She never measured the value of the painting. Not ever.

Violet followed her father back to the table and found Jack sipping her Bee's Knees. His gaze was worried as it moved from Violet to her father and then back to Vi. She smiled slightly at him and then at her father. Only her father believed her expression was not a lie.

Violet returned to her seat. "What can you tell us about Mr. Rees' family?" she asked calmly though her insides were still jittery.

"There's the sister. The Stevens woman you apparently met. Jack told me," he added. "There are several sons. I think they're all married. Perhaps a daughter. There is a new generation of grandchildren. I believe that he lost his wife a few years ago. I suppose that any of them might be expecting to receive something."

Violet's stomach was too sour for the cocktail, and she rubbed her brow before sipping from her water. "Must it only be family?"

"He died in his home around the holidays," her father replied. "I would suspect that several good friends could have been visiting as well."

Her father glanced at her meaningfully as Vi's own house was full of friends during Christmas.

"Perhaps," Violet agreed.

"Olly was a friend of mine and his friends are mine as well. I'll track his closest down at my club to see what we can find out about who might have been there."

Violet sighed. All that would do was give them a list of who could have killed the old man. Her father, though, was not shying away from involving himself in the matter, even agreeing quickly that it had to be murder, which told Violet that she hadn't been foolish to pursue this.

"Where did he die?"

"He was found dead in his bed." The earl shuddered. "The indignity of killing a man in his bed. It's not to be born."

Violet's dark look had him shuffling a bit.

"It is cruel to kill a man in his bed. One wants to be shot down—some sort of warrior's death—or die peacefully surrounded by your children." Jack's comment was an attempt to smooth things between father and daughter but it was unsuccessful.

Both of them were too stubborn for that. The tension between them hadn't faded in months and Violet supposed that it would eventually die a long, lingering death. Violet tried a smile, but even the earl could see it was a false attempt.

Finally, she said, "I haven't been myself since we got back to London."

"Are you well?" he asked her with a concern that she was catty enough to enjoy. She hated that she needed these little signs that he cared about her, but she did. Her sister, Isolde, never worried in the least about proof of their father's love. Nor did Gerald, her oldest brother. It was the burden of Violet, her twin Victor, and their youngest brother, Geoffrey.

"I'm fine," Violet told him. She cast Jack a harsh look and then sipped her water once again to avoid speaking further.

"That was a telling glance your way, Jack. What did you do? Can't you buy her flowers or jewelry and move this stage along?"

Jack winced as Violet's gaze narrowed on her father. He didn't seem to feel the effect, but Jack knew her too well to not see what was happening behind her even expression.

"I'm afraid it's not so simple," Jack said and then added, "and best not discussed over drinks any more than what happened to her aunt."

The earl lifted his brows, glanced between them, and then said, "My apologies." He stood and then leaned down, dropping a casual kiss on Violet's forehead. "I'll see what I can find out. Meet me at my club later, Jack, and I'll fill you in."

Vi's husband nodded as her father left. She didn't miss that he'd ordered her husband to the gentlemen's club rather than coming by their house or sending for them at his home. Violet hid her hurt and turned to Jack.

He had also turned her direction. "Did you sleep at all?"

Vi bit down on her bottom lip. "It seems that telling yourself to calm down and let things go isn't as easy as doing so. My nighttime mind completely ignored my instructions."

Jack's laugh didn't make her feel better, but the twinkle in his eyes did.

"Why do you love me when I'm full of madness?"

"It makes life spicy," he grinned evilly and she nudged his leg under the table.

"Does it?" She scowled at him, but she meant it for herself.

Had she slept? No. She'd tossed and turned and worried and hated him and loved him and wondered why things seemed so dark all the time when they were endlessly bright for others. Lila never saw the gray days. Victor—who had shared a womb with Violet—never felt the gray days. Jack seemed to see the darkness and yet it never touched him the way it suffocated her.

Why did she wake on days where she should be happy and feel as though she were in a black cloud? Why did she suffer when so many others didn't? And how did she find her way out of it? Instead of pouring all of that on him, she forced herself to grin. "Just because my mind, heart, and imagination don't align as I tell them to."

"You never were one for following orders," he told her, lifting her hand and kissing the back of it, "not even from yourself."

They lingered over drinks before Jack excused himself for some appointment or other. He was probably stepping into Scotland Yard for a meeting that Violet would just as soon not hear about. She let him go without asking him further questions, and for doing so, he pressed a kiss on her head and whispered his love.

CHAPTER 5

*J*ack took Violet home and left to join her father. She considered going back to bed and pulling the blankets over her head, but she was afraid it would take her weeks to get out of bed again. So, she paced the drawing room, putting things away, rearranging little knick-knacks and eyeing the valuables they left causally lying about.

"Was that what killed Olly Rees?"

No one was there to answer her and Violet felt keenly the lack of her friends. Lila and Denny were at Victor's country house, refusing to move until their baby was born. Kate and Victor were held captive by poor Kate's endless sicking up. Rita had returned to Scotland with her father and taken Ham along. Even her ward, Ginny, was back at school.

"Did some poor relative, struggling to survive," she said aloud to her non-present friends, "walk into the man's home and see the casual wealth? See a way to escape their poverty? Is our killer someone who didn't love Olly and was simply jealous?"

Violet could imagine it too easily. She had been the poor, struggling relative, but the idea of murder would have never crossed her mind.

It could as easily be that Olly Rees knew of a crime that the murderer kept hidden. Maybe he was murdered over what he knew? Maybe he was murdered for God knows what reason. How could she guess? The Reeses were complete strangers, so guessing might as well be trying to figure out the killer at the end of an Agatha Christie book she hadn't read.

Violet called for Hargreaves and asked him to telephone Phoebe Rees. Perhaps a girls' day of shopping would be enough to pull Violet from the megrims and give her an idea of what in the world had been happening at the Rees home during the holidays that had led to the death of an energetic old man.

VIOLET INVITED Phoebe to her favorite boutique and the woman came despite being large with child, a shape the boutique didn't cater to.

"I am sorry about Aunt Stevens," Phoebe said as she took a seat near the dressing room. "She was quite awful. Sometimes I think she's a little batty, stirring up trouble and seeing things that aren't there."

Violet stepped out of the room in a dark blue dress edged with gold. She turned in the mirrors and looked at the shop girl. "No. It's too big." To Phoebe, Violet said, "I can't really say it's all right, can I? I won't. She jabbed me right where it would hurt the most while she popped a petit four into her mouth."

Violet didn't, however, agree with the batty assessment. Perhaps, past feeling sympathy for those who were struggling, but not batty. It was a clever woman who knew where to jab and make it hurt.

"She's a hateful old thing. Grandfather Rees was lovely. His sister is sour and likes to watch you squirm. Then just as quickly she turns and is kind. So you never know what to expect. It makes one quite twisty. I would rather she be cruel all the time rather than kind then cruel then kind then back again. If you knew she was going to be awful, you could go in with your shield raised."

Violet took a deep breath in, glancing back as she asked casually, "So who do you think killed Olly Rees?"

Phoebe's mouth dropped open and she shook her head. "Killed him? He was old."

"But showing no sign of illness." Violet realized that as she pursued a puzzle, the greyness faded. Her heart lightening at the coming dawn of happiness that felt selfish considering she was discussing a man's death. It had begun earlier when she paced the drawing room, talking aloud to no one. Her mind had found a focus and she wasn't going to let it drop easily. "If someone were to have killed him, why would they do so?"

Phoebe stared at Violet as though she'd gone mad and then slowly answered, "I don't know."

"Oh just guess," Vi prompted. How hard was it to throw out an idea during a gossip session.

"I don't know. I don't think he was murdered. Why would I ponder on that?"

Violet's mouth twisted as she faced Phoebe. "But you did like him?"

Phoebe nodded as if Violet were stupid. "Of course I did. He was a kind old man. My husband has endless stories about how wonderful he was. Grandfather Olly would take his grandsons out for these long hikes and talk to them about his early days. In fact, he never left out his granddaughter. You can be sure that everyone else isn't as careful to love my Alice as they are to love my sister-in-law's sons."

Violet lifted a brow and Phoebe shrugged.

"Don't look at me like that," Phoebe snapped. "I'd be happy to just have a couple of daughters."

"But your husband? he adores Grandfather Olly?"

Phoebe nodded, clearly bored with the conversation. "Yes, yes. Olly would walk and talk and tell the stories of his parents and grandparents. Harold loved the stories. He couldn't wait for another long walk with Olly. When he missed that final walk with Olly when Olly went with Charlotte and not Harold, he was jealous like a small child."

Violet took the next dress from the shop girl. "Olly sounds wonderful."

"He was," Phoebe sniffled not losing the edge of boredom. "I miss the old boy. He used to call me 'my pretty.' Hello my pretty,' he'd say. Then he'd take my hand and kiss me as if I were stepping out with him onto a ballroom floor."

"What a lovely memory," Violet said quietly. "I do think I'd have liked him."

"Harold wants to name the baby Olly, but I th-think it's a girl."

Violet took a breath in. She didn't want to get drawn into a discussion of babies and pregnancy. "Olivia is an excellent name. Olly would be an adorable nickname for her."

"I hate being pregnant," Phoebe moaned. "My sister loves it. She glows. She's a shining star of beauty who doesn't seem to feel the burden at all. I feel like I'm being suffocated by my own body."

"What about Grandfather Olly?" Violet asked, disregarding Phoebe's list of woes at her state. "Is there any reason to believe someone could have killed him?"

"Won't you let it go?" Phoebe groaned, rubbing her belly and then scowling around the shop that didn't cater to her needs.

Violet shook her head. "I can't."

"Why?" Phoebe stared at Violet. "You have everything. Why dig into our mess when you can do whatever you want."

"You could?" Violet asked.

Phoebe scoffed and shook her head. "Your Jack clearly lets you do whatever you want. Harold isn't quite so generous. He's a bit jealous to be honest. I suppose I should be happy he still wants me to be his rather than not caring at all."

Oh, Violet didn't agree with that at all, but she hid her thoughts.

Phoebe's tirade continued with, "How long have you been married? And you aren't carrying a baby yet? You can't do that without his help," she added as though Violet hadn't the first idea about how to go about attaining motherhood.

"We haven't been married long," Violet answered simply.

"Surely...before..."

"It's not really any of your business." Violet took the dress back into the dressing room, dropped the new one over her head and returned to the trifold of mirrors and Phoebe, knowing she was being a hypocrite when she continued her questioning. Surely it wasn't any of her business, either, what had happened in the Rees family. Except someone wanted her involved. "What about your sisters-in-law? You don't seem to like each other much."

"There's Delilah and Charlotte. Delilah—well, you saw. Having my daughter made Delilah jealous and it's worse now. Technically, she's a cousin-in-law, but they might as well all be siblings. Delilah wants nothing more than a houseful of babies, so of course, I am the one who has one after another while her cradle is empty. Charlotte has four little ones, but her little children are all with her overseas most of the time, so Delilah doesn't envy Charlotte quite the same way."

Violet took a long breath in to hold back a stern reprimand. It wasn't that Violet disagreed with Phoebe, it was more that her tone was so unkind. "It must be hard to see others have children and want them so badly yourself," Violet said gently.

Phoebe shrugged rather callously and then added, "It's not my fault, but she makes it seem as though it is. I find it harder and harder to care given her nasty asides. She takes every scrap of joy and twists it. She even tries to steal my Alice's heart. I wouldn't be surprised if she whispered to Alice that I wanted her to be a boy."

"Would she have killed Grandfather Olly?"

"I don't know," Phoebe groaned, clearly tired of the line of questions. "Why would anyone kill him? He gave his children an education. He was a good man. There isn't enough money to change anything for anyone and spur them into the evil through their greed. He was a good man, who was loved by his family."

Violet winced. "Then why?"

"Maybe," Phoebe said begrudgingly, "it wasn't about money." It was the closest Phoebe came to suggesting his death hadn't been natural.

Violet stared at Phoebe and then said agreed, slowly, "Maybe it wasn't about money."

VIOLET BOUGHT dresses almost absently as she gossiped with Phoebe. Her old school friend refused to be pulled back into a conversation about Olly Rees, but Violet was eventually able to ask her about where she lived and what they did.

"Oh," Phoebe grinned brightly. "We live here in London, thank goodness."

Violet asked about her rooms and Harold's work and what she did with her days and before asking, "Did your grandfather live alone?"

"Oh yes, Aunt Stevens has been living with Grandfather Olly for some time."

Violet glanced a question that begged for elaboration.

"When her husband died, she said the empty home made her sad, though Harold and I assumed she wanted to live with her brother because she's a penny-pincher."

"Is she? That house party she's speaking of doesn't sound anything like penny-pinching."

"Oh," Phoebe grinned wickedly. "She spends money. She just wants to spend it on being important and lording it around a bit. I don't mind so much if it keeps her from being too nasty." Phoebe laughed and then suggested, "That red scarf would go so well with the red dress you bought."

Violet examined it before she scrunched her nose and asked, "You don't mind her lording about?"

"She does so in a way that's generous and benefits my family. When she isn't tossing about her cruel little taunts, she can be a fun old broad."

Violet grinned as if she were interested in the gossip and not delving into the intricacies of the family with the intent of trying to determine whether Grandfather Olly had been murdered and who might have had a reason to do so.

Phoebe didn't appear to notice the subtle direction of Violet's questions or she surely would have stopped the conversation. Instead she nodded towards a passing woman and asked, "Doesn't she look like Tara Longfellow? Oh I did hate her in school."

"She was a handful," Violet agreed. "I was always convinced she went through my things whenever I wasn't in my room."

"She did," Phoebe said with a dark look. "I caught her twice leaving other girl's rooms. I even started heading up early from lunch to catch her. She finally stopped searching it then, and I never found her new timeframe, but I found my things rifled enough to be sure someone had."

"I did too!" Violet agreed. "I thought about trying to catch them, but other than infuriating me, I was busy with other things. I just ended up locking my trunk with anything that was private."

Phoebe glanced over at Vi and then added, "I did the same. And I left out nonsense to confuse her."

Violet fluffed her hair in the mirror and then asked, "Aside from Delilah's issue with you—"

"Which is not my fault, but she makes it seem as though it is," Phoebe interrupted.

Violet bit down on her bottom lip and then continued. "What about the other women in your family? Do they upset her as well?"

"How can they as easily?" Phoebe sniffed. "For me, Delilah and I are both in London. Charlotte, Harold's sister, is normally out of the country traveling with her missionary husband. Delilah isn't watching babies grow, is she? They're just amorphous ideas for the most part. Whereas my little one is in Delilah's presence, prancing about being herself and Delilah seems to take it as a personal insult."

"Are there no other members of the family around?"

"There was only Olly and Aunt Stevens in their generation. Aunt Stevens didn't have any children. Olly had two sons and they each had two. Harold and Charlotte on the one side. Joseph and Alexander for the second son. Alexander isn't married, but you've met Delilah, Joseph's wife."

"So Harold's father inherits Olly's house?" Violet asked idly as if she weren't trying to ferret things out. "Will Mrs. Stevens need to relocate?"

Phoebe shook her head. "No, no. Use of the house

was left to Aunt Stevens while she lives. Harold's father has his own house that is equally nice." She eyed Violet askance and said, "I'm not stupid you know. I realize you're sleuthing. I'm just not sure why."

"Curiosity," Violet lied. Was it Phoebe who had left the note in Violet's house? Was she, perhaps, just pretending to be unaware as to why Violet was so curious? Violet hooked her arm through Phoebe's and asked, "Dessert?"

CHAPTER 6

*V*iolet returned to her house thinking she remembered why she'd liked Phoebe well enough and had also never missed her during the holiday breaks. Vi found Jack inside the house, smoking in the parlor, and scowled at him from where she stood in the great hall.

"I bought oodles of dresses." Her tone was deliberately sour.

"Fabulous," he said idly, reading through her act. "Did you jump in any puddles?"

Vi had to turn her head to hide her sudden grin. When she had her face under control, she shot him a dark look before letting Hargreaves take her coat. She longed to curl up next to Jack. Spending the day shopping with someone other than Lila, Rita, or Kate was exhausting.

"Would you like some coffee, Mrs. Vi?"

She nodded and winked at Hargreaves to let him

know she was playing before crossing to Jack. She loomed over him with her hands on her hips. "Puddles? What is this madness? Why would anyone do such a thing?"

Jack set his cigarette aside. "Is that how you want to play this?"

Vi tried an innocent expression, but it didn't work. She tried to emulate her dogs when they wanted a treat, but he was unmoved. He lifted a brow at her and she reached out to push it back down with her forefinger.

Jack took her by her hips and pulled her onto his lap. "Are you done yet?"

"Sirrah!" she gasped. "Whatever do you mean?"

"You know exactly what I mean," he said gently. He looked her over as though he were reading a book and she noticed the way his jaw loosened and his shoulders relaxed. She was reading him as easily as he was reading her. "You're feeling better."

"Perhaps a puzzle like Olly Rees' death is enough of a diversion for me to be distracted from whatever else is going on inside my head. Or perhaps the reason why I'm —I don't know? Broken? Is that the right word?"

Jack shook his head. With a low voice he said, "It is not. You are not broken. Not in the least. You are extraordinary."

Violet rolled her eyes and Jack cupped her cheeks holding her gaze on his. She was bare before him even though she was fully dressed. It was more uncomfortable than being naked. "Perhaps the main part of my problem is simply that I am without purpose."

"Without purpose?" Jack frowned. "I don't see you that way."

"I feel that way. Like I'm only wandering through life, bored and purposeless," Violet scowled. "It's not that I haven't always struggled with grey days. It's just now I don't have the distraction of the business things for Aunt Agatha anymore. I write, but it doesn't have the same hunger now that I don't need the money from the books to live. I don't have children nor am I ready for them. I—I can do whatever I want and what I find is that I struggle to want to do anything."

Jack, unlike everyone else, didn't look at her as though her woes were ridiculous. She knew they were. She knew that across London other women were struggling to survive day-by-day. Those women worked hard to eat, to dress themselves, to care for their children. Violet wanted nothing more than her own life of ease.

She was well aware that struggling to be happy when you had everything was idiotic but that just made her feelings all the more difficult to carry. It was like there was something inside of her heart and mind that was amiss and being unable to share and have another person understand what was going on left her feeling lonelier than before.

"Darling Vi," Jack said, kissing her forehead. "I don't have any idea what to say."

She turned to face him, seeing the worry in his eyes and it made her feel even more of a failure. They spent so much of their lives together and she found herself having moments and days of drowning in an inexplicable darkness.

"Does it help to know that I love you?"

She nodded, leaning forward to press her forehead against his.

"Then know that I do."

They curled into each other until Hargreaves knocked on the door with coffee and after he left, Violet took a seat next to Jack on the Chesterfield and leaned into his side. She still felt better but there was a frantic need inside of her to figure out why she felt so grey on her bad days.

"Will you love me if I'm like this for the rest of our lives?" she asked him, and a fervent kiss was her answer.

VIOLET AND JACK dressed for the scavenger hunt with care.

"The last time they did this," Jack told her as he pulled on boots and started lacing them, "people ended in the lost tunnels of the underground. I don't think that pretty, grey dress will be sufficient, Vi."

He wore a tan sporting suit with black pinstripe lines on the trousers and vest that crossed into squares. The jacket was the same tan without pinstripes. He wore a blue shirt under his vest with a darker blue tie. With his sporting boots, he looked like the most attractive man on the sporting range she could imagine.

Violet grinned wickedly. She had been saving a joke for him for a while, but now it was both practical and funny. She went to her dressing room and dug to the back of the closet. Vi had joined Victor the last time he'd gone shopping and ordered a sporting suit for herself that matched her twin's. Hers wasn't as simple as Jack's. Instead, she had gotten a flashy plaid suit. It was tan, deep brown, and a deep red, but the tan was the overwhelming color, so she wouldn't clash with Jack too much.

Violet put it on, with the brown dress shirt and the red tie. She'd bought boots that matched Victor's, just as the suit did. She pulled the wool socks up to the knees, added the boots she'd been breaking in secretly and then adjusted a matching cap over her hair. When she was finished, she leaned against the doorway of their bedroom from the dressing room with her hands in the vest pockets.

Jack glanced her way and his shout of laughter made the secret all worthwhile. She walked across their room as though she were walking a catwalk and then spun as she reached the bedroom door. She fluffed the ends of her hair. "I think this outfit needs my spider ring."

"And," Jack said, casually handing her a black velvet box, "perhaps a little something more."

Violet lifted a brow in question.

It took him a moment to answer the unspoken inquiry that hung between them. "I did nothing wrong. I thought I'd follow your father's advice. Throw a little jewelry your way and brighten your day."

Vi snorted and he admitted, "When I went out today, you were on my mind and I saw those and imagined them on you. I have to admit, I was thinking more of one of your slinky evening dresses."

Violet slowly opened the box and found diamond and pearl chandelier earbobs. The pearls were unique brown pearls and the rose gold would go well with her suit. She put them on with a smile and then crossed to Jack's dresser and took out one of the tie pins to add to her tie.

She examined herself in the mirror. "I am a pretty boy."

Jack's laugh was followed by a dry comment. "We already knew that. Stretch you out a bit and subtract some of my favorite attributes, and you're the image of Victor."

Vi adjusted her vest over her chest. "These attributes and my fabulous suit are going to be victorious in this scavenger hunt."

Vi put a spiral broach on her jacket lapel, added a thick layer of brick red lipstick that matched her suit and thickened the rouge on her cheeks. She had no intention of appearing as anything other than a woman who just happened to be wearing a suit.

"Are you ready?" Violet asked Jack, who put on his overcoat.

"You need a coat as well, darling. It hasn't stopped being January, and it's cold and wet outside."

"Yes, of course," Violet agreed. She looked through her coats before choosing a red wool coat. It reached her knees and accented her suit. "I love you even when you mother-hen me. But I might deserve it for hopping in puddles while wearing a dress the other day."

"Do you think so?" Jack asked idly, but his eyes were grinning at her, and she grinned back at him.

"Possibly. Of course, what you deserve for getting injured is a whole list unto itself, so be careful how you use your digs."

Jack wrapped an arm around her waist and lifted her to press a kiss against her temple.

"Careful, darling," she warned. "I have man boots now. So much easier to do damage with."

Jack's huff of laughter made her grin into his neck before he slid her down his body and suggested, "We could stay home."

"We're going to win this thing."

"You don't care about winning."

"We're going to join a bunch of spoiled acquaintances and have delightful food and drinks and then wander London throughout the night and go to an Indian restaurant at 5:00 am where we'll have paneer tikka masala and naan before we collapse into bed like the spoiled, useless, bright young things we are."

Jack pressed another kiss into her temple. "Smith is going to drive us."

"Smith? Shady private detective Smith? The one that has weaseled his life into my Beatrice's heart?"

Jack shook his head. "I think he's using us as cover for another of his cases."

"Or preparing to rob everyone we know there."

"That too," Jack agreed.

CHAPTER 7

*V*iolet and Jack approached the statue of Peter Pan with a mass of others. Some were in cocktail dresses and fine suits, others were dressed like Jack and had sporty-looking women on their arms who weren't dressed nearly as enthusiastically sporty or masculine as Violet was in her suit. Then there was the trio of women wearing thick mink coats and dripping in jewels.

Violet sighed deeply when she spotted the pregnant Phoebe on the arm of a man with a somewhat familiar face. Delilah Rees and another man that Vi assumed was Delilah's husband was with them. There was another fellow, of the same age, and who looked so much like Phoebe and Delilah's husbands that Violet felt certain this was Delilah's brother-in-law. What had Phoebe called him? Alan? No, Violet thought, Alexander. It was noteworthy, really, how much those three Rees men looked alike. Violet wasn't an identical twin, obviously, but her twin looked like the masculine version of her. These three looked only slightly less alike than Violet and Victor.

"Don't look now," Violet told Jack though he knew none of them, "but it's the Rees cousins and their wives."

Jack's eyes closed in frustration. "This was supposed to be fun and entirely uninvolved in murder."

"It will be," Violet said, consolingly. "Don't make eye contact."

"Violet, my beautiful darling, you're dressed like a man and gathering attention in that dashing suit. There's no way that you will avoid their attention."

Vi pressed up on her toes and kissed his chin. "Then, we'll be discovered, but we can still have fun. I apologize for being so flashy."

Jack glanced at Violet and then at the statue where a man wearing what looked like a circus ringmaster outfit was handing out envelopes. "We could go do something just as foolish without all of these hangers on. We don't need them to…to…"

"Engage in hijinks?" Violet asked, running her finger along his jawline.

"Exactly. Let's go explore the Underground ourselves. We can find the lost tunnels."

"Or play a series of guess-where for our own private scavenger hunt."

Jack guessed, "Wellington Arch."

She groaned since it was what she'd been thinking of. She shot back, "Big Ben."

He took the envelope from the ringmaster and a moment later a finger tapped Jack's back near Violet's hand. He stiffened under her fingers and turned, keeping Violet behind him protectively as usual. She peeked around his shoulder to find a laughing Phoebe holding a bottle of wine. She was half-drunk and her husband was mostly holding her up while she laughed into his neck.

"Violet! Violet, my favorite chum! Meet Harold again! He's so fat!"

Violet curtsied in her suit. "So nice to meet you."

He frowned at her. "Phoebe said you were elegant."

"Sometimes," Violet said lightly.

"Violet," Phoebe laughed and then staggered into Jack, who caught her and nudged her towards her husband, "thinks Grandfather Olly was murdered."

Her husband froze, as did the other members of her party, while Phoebe giggled into her hand.

Jack cleared his throat and tugged Violet under his arm as the two cousins focused furious gazes on her.

"Why would you think that?" demanded Delilah's husband while Harold pulled Phoebe back up. The brother, Alexander, looked between both couples and then raised his hand to a few fellows who called his name, leaving behind his brother, his cousin, and both of their wives and not even looking back. He had no reaction to the claim of murder. His disgust was mainly for Harold and Phoebe.

"We received an anonymous letter that claimed so," Jack told them flatly. "For the love of heaven man, pick up your wife and carry her. She's going to break an ankle."

Violet let Jack tuck her closer, knowing the anger of the other gents was setting off all his protective instincts. Phoebe was still giggling drunkenly, but Delilah looked disgusted and self-righteous at the same time, given she too was carrying a bottle of wine.

"Why does your Aunt Stevens suspect her brother was murdered?" Violet asked them.

"She doesn't!" Delilah gasped. She glanced down at her bottle of wine and then shot Violet another dark look without taking a sip. And there, Violet thought, was the difference between Delilah and Phoebe.

"She's an old woman who has nothing," Harold shot back cruelly. "She's bored and alone and only important to herself."

Violet winced and glanced at Jack, who couldn't pull Violet any closer, so instead he just spread his hand wider over her side as though one of these spoiled idiots were about to pull a knife and lunge at them.

"Losing Grandfather was bad enough," Delilah's husband, Joseph, said. "Why do we have to relive it again because of the fantasies of some idle, bored old woman?"

"It wasn't her who left the note at our house. Many of your grandfather's friends think the same. It is very likely that one of you knows Olly Rees was murdered and you're trying to bully everyone else into thinking otherwise."

Delilah's husband took her by the arm and pulled her back. "Let's get out of here, Dee. I'm not surprised some old friend of Phoebe's is crazy." His expression was exasperated both with Violet and Phoebe, and Violet was tempted to take him by the ear, force him to read the anonymous letter, and then point out that she—at least—wasn't stumbling drunk.

Violet snorted as Jack stiffened.

"Careful now," Jack said. Joseph looked Jack over,

noting his mountainous shoulder, thick biceps, and furious gaze and held up his hands in surrender.

Phoebe gasped long after everyone else had winced over the insult. "Are you insulting her by using me? Joseph, you are just mean." To her husband she slurred, "I never liked Joseph. He's always so nasty. Delilah should have done better. Maybe if she'd shaken Joseph off instead of marrying him, she'd have a baby and stop being so jealous about ours."

Her husband set her down and snapped, "Phoebe. Be quiet! That's enough."

Vi lifted a brow at the dressing down worthy of a school girl.

"No!" Phoebe cried, shaking off his arm and stumbling away. She nearly fell before she caught herself. Stopping to sway until she gathered her balance and then lean carefully down. She put her arms out in an obvious attempt to keep herself on her feet while she pulled off her shoes, throwing them at her husband. "You always take her side! Delilah's mean to me and you take her side and you never appreciate what I do. You...you...snake in the grass!"

"Oh, there she goes again," Delilah said. The coldness of her words had Violet wincing because Delilah disguised it as gentle empathy to Phoebe's husband. Violet knew women like Delilah far too well. The overt attempt to show the difference between them was just a nasty way to draw attention to Delilah's positives and elucidate Phoebe's negatives.

The precision of the meanness was worse, in Violet's opinion. She'd rather have an out-and-out nasty woman face off with her than someone who pretended to be your friend until you were looking the other way.

Phoebe staggered away and then she turned back. "I never should have married you, Harold Rees. My mama was so right."

Phoebe's husband threw his hands in the air and walked off in the other direction. He was chased by Delilah while her husband looked at the stumbling Phoebe and then at his wife and Harold heading the other way. There was a momentary glance towards his brother, Alexander, but he was already gone with his group of friends.

"Harold, you can't let Phoebe go that way," Joseph called. "It's not safe. She's far too into her cups."

Harold didn't turn and neither did Delilah. Joseph groaned and then chased after Phoebe.

"They're delightful," Jack said dryly. "We should certainly accept any house party invitations their bored and unimportant aunt sends. That wouldn't be a terrible idea at all."

"Let's follow them," Violet suggested.

Jack stared at her.

"Follow Delilah and Harold," she clarified. "Phoebe is about ten minutes from crying into hands and then falling asleep on the couch."

"Why them?" Jack asked as Violet started towards the path where the other two had disappeared into the darkness.

"Delilah and Harold aren't drunk. Joseph is only going to be persuading Phoebe into an auto and home. He'll be carrying her snoring self into her bedroom and dumping her on the bed with her shoes still on before he goes home since he won't know where Harold and Delilah went off to."

Jack shrugged and followed Violet, hurrying enough to take her hand while they disappeared down the paths of the park. Jack suddenly tugged her into a stand of trees, placing a hand over her mouth as he pulled her deeper into the darkness.

She jerked her mouth free and then whispered low, "What do you see with those eyes of yours?"

"Delilah and Harold are fighting. Passionately."

"Fighting?" Violet pressed up on her toes, but she just didn't have the height Jack did. "Why?" Violet muffled her irritation into his chest. A moment later, she said, "He really is a snake in the grass. That Delilah is too. Why are they fighting? Did they kill the grandfather? Is that why they're fighting?"

"They could be fighting about anything, Vi. About having killed the grandfather. About the fact that Harold let Phoebe get drunk and storm off. About some long term issue we know nothing about."

Violet shook her head in frustration. "Let's leave it, why don't we? Let's leave the madness and do the scavenger hunt. Open the hint. It's Big Ben, isn't it?"

Jack didn't open the hint. "Cocktails and paneer," he suggested instead.

"Yes," Violet agreed immediately. "Absolutely. I'm in. That's a much better idea. Then let's do something adventurous, because I'm dressed for hijinks not dancing."

Jack laughed and pulled her close to him. "I'm glad you don't think I'm a snake in the grass."

"I'm glad you would take better care of me when I'm zozzled than Harold does of Phoebe."

Jack tilted her face to him and gently placed a kiss on each eye before he added, "There's nothing like being around people who are horrible to make us grateful for what we have, is there?"

Violet nodded and followed him back to where Smith had left the auto. He wasn't there.

"Shall we leave him?" Violet asked.

"Yes, of course," Jack laughed. "Smith is more resourceful than the two of us put together. I never expected him to do anything other than drive us here and disappear at some point during this scavenger hunt."

Jack started the auto and they left Smith and the Rees family. As they drove, Violet asked, "What did you and Father find out about Rees from his friend?"

"Are we doing this? Are we going to keep diving in?"

Violet looked at him and then back at the dark, rainy road. "Aren't you curious?"

Jack shrugged and then admitted, "Yes, but I don't like them, and nothing makes me feel more like a failure than not saving your aunt. This case has all the earmarks of that one, Violet."

"Nothing makes me feel like a terrible niece and worthless human more than having failed to save Aunt Agatha as well, Jack. In the end, it was her choice not to leave. Why couldn't I persuade her to go? Why couldn't I, who loved her, get her to leave? To be safe? If she had left, we'd have had time to figure out who was trying to hurt her and stop Meredith."

Jack squeezed Violet's hand. "I could really use paneer

tikka masala and naan and something so spicy my nose burns."

"If it burns enough," Violet agreed, "maybe it will distract us from failing Aunt Agatha."

"And those Rees idiots."

"And how all of our friends are moving so foolishly ahead of us."

Jack snorted at her and kissed the back of her hand. "Having babies before we do makes it easier for us to learn from their mistakes and to steal the best nanny later."

"I miss them," Violet said with a sigh. "Even though Denny is lazy and sometimes mean and Kate is sick. Victor—"

Violet trailed off. She and her brother had been separated over a lifetime of being in different schools, but she still never felt right in her skin when he was too far away and not easy to speak to.

"And missing the babies," Jack said to distract her from her brother. "I know."

CHAPTER 8

*V*iolet found Beatrice in her office. "I'm bored. I don't know what to do with myself anymore."

Beatrice looked up in alarm as Violet flopped onto the chair opposite. Her former maid turned secretary turned business manager almost certainly didn't want to be a maid again and Violet could see the fear in her friend's gaze.

"I'm not ready to become a businesswoman again, Beatrice," Violet assured her friend. "You do wonderful in meetings and reading dry reports and sleuthing information about business investments that I can't possibly stand to return to."

Beatrice's relief was palpable and her shoulders relaxed.

"You are, however, very smart. Wise even."

Beatrice paused in horror, staring at Violet as if poor

Beatrice were about to be asked to do something terrible. Quietly, she asked, "What does that mean?"

"It means that I could use some advice."

Beatrice's gaze widened further as Violet gestured to the maid in the doorway and had her bring in a tray. A small teapot, a small coffee pot, a plate of nibbles. Violet poured them both a cup as if they were just friends instead of employer and employee. For Violet's part, she'd happily called Beatrice her friend. Beatrice, however, had been raised to see Violet as 'better' and the former maid was having trouble bypassing that early instruction.

"Violet," Beatrice started. "I—"

Vi grinned when Beatrice didn't stumble over her name and lifted her coffee cup in salute.

"I don't have any idea what you should do," Beatrice finished.

"Work for me," Smith said from the doorway. "You have the poor-mes when you're bored. I could use a ritzy woman like you to help me with my cases."

"Why not Beatrice?" Violet asked immediately, taking in the pretty-as-an-angel private detective. A moment later she asked, "Do you have the run of my house?"

"Beatrice is too honest." he said to the first question. To the second he just shot her a scathing look. Of course he had the run of her house, she thought.

Violet realized she didn't mind all that much and laughed while Beatrice gasped. "Violet work for you? Are you mad? Do you want Jack to murder you slowly? Slowly and viciously?"

"Just an idea," Smith said, eyeing Violet with something that said he'd help her get into trouble. "Consider it revoked."

It was clear that he didn't mean it would be revoked. His gaze turned to Beatrice and even though absolutely nothing changed about his expression or body, he still seemed to soften for just a smidgeon of a breath. His gaze was a mask once again when it returned to Violet. "You're excellent at interfering in people's lives and helping them along the way. Why don't you...I don't know...why don't you find girls like your Ginny and change their lives like you did hers? She's a scrapper. Now she's a scrapper with money and a future."

Beatrice immediately shook her head.

"Why not?" Smith demanded. "That was nearly as good of an idea as working for me."

"Vi's imagination is too specific for that. She'll unfold a story for every girl she meets. The ones who don't want to be helped? For Violet, she'd dream up the worst scenario. There are other ways to find a driving purpose that doesn't include your happiness being linked to the poor decision-making skills of scrappers who aren't as bright as Ginny." Beatrice shot him a look that told him to be quiet as she added, "And working for you was the worst idea I've ever heard."

Smith's shrug said he didn't care one way or the other. He looked between the women and muttered something about being back later. Violet watched him go and then turned her gaze to Beatrice.

Beatrice flushed brilliantly. "I'm sorry. I promise he doesn't interfere in my work. I'm afraid I've told him time and again to not come by while I'm working, but—" She shook her head helplessly. "I seem to be unsuccessful at convincing him to respect any sort of boundaries."

The avalanche of excuses came to a stop when Violet reached out and took Beatrice's hand. "I don't care, Beatrice. I wouldn't have you in charge of my finances if I didn't trust you completely. Take a long lunch with Smith. Go for walks and have a break. Let him bring you flowers and, I don't know, nuzzle your neck. I am not going to count your every minute working for me."

Beatrice's blush, which had been strong before, was fiery and Violet's chuckle didn't help in the least.

"I can see why you like him." Violet sipped her coffee to enjoy Beatrice's squirming.

"He's too pretty for his own good. Or mine."

Violet laughed low and wicked and then shoved the nibbles towards her friend, who looked on the edge of fainting. Perhaps she needed to occupy her hands and mouth with a scone. Beatrice seemed to agree as she split it and topped it with clotted cream and jam with trembling hands.

"He is too pretty for all of mankind," Violet agreed. "When you first see him, you think heaven sent down one of her most beautiful angels and then you realize he's in the devil's pocket."

"Yet somehow," Beatrice muttered dryly, "he still convinces you to trust him. Despite knowing what he is. The whole time you're scolding yourself all the while trusting him implicitly."

"He does! You know that slew of private investigators that I hired when those fools at Scotland Yard thought that Jack killed Theodophilus? Smith is the only one that I've hired regularly. Why? The other fellows are much more principled. But when I need something done? I call Smith."

Beatrice nodded. "I think half of his work comes from old men who think their young wives are cuckolding them. They assume he'll use his pretty face to lead them into a trap."

"Does he?" Violet asked, knowing he didn't. Beatrice wouldn't be interested in a man who spent his days in such a way.

"No," Beatrice said. "No, he wouldn't. He's not like that."

Violet nodded, making sure her friend saw that Vi was unsurprised by the answer. If Violet had her way, Beatrice would continue to be a regular part of Vi's family. If Smith had his way, Beatrice would be his. He was the kind of man to want every aspect of the woman he loved. He'd want her heart, her imagination, her body, her home, but Violet didn't think it was a bad thing in a man who gave all of that in return.

She rubbed her finger over her bottom lip, wondering if she was crediting Smith too much. Anxiety for Beatrice rose in Violet and then she realized, it wasn't something she could control. Beatrice was careful and precise. It was why she'd been an excellent maid, and it was why she moved from position to position with Violet.

Careful, smart, precise. It was all that you could want for your friend. Violet hoped, in fact, that those good attributes didn't keep Beatrice from throwing her heart to the wind and living fully.

Violet took a biscuit and broke it to pieces as Beatrice ran over updates on the business side of things. Vi was only half-listening, but she caught enough to feel sure that Beatrice's thoughts were a good way to go. Vi popped one of the broken biscuit pieces in her mouth and then sipped her coffee again.

"We've been drawn into another murder," Violet said when Beatrice finished. Her business manager paused, looking up with wide eyes that were filled with concern. "An old man that someone thinks was murdered by a member of his family."

Beatrice's gaze turned sad. "Like Mrs. Davies?"

Violet nodded. Yes, just like her aunt. Too much like her aunt.

"Oh Vi," Beatrice said, and it was her turn to reach out and take Vi's hands over the desk. "You don't have to do this. You don't have to relive what happened to your aunt or let it all be churned up again."

Violet's eyes welled. "I know. But I can't help but want to. I can't help but think that no one is really fighting for that old man, and Olly Rees seemed like a good old fellow."

"Like your aunt," Beatrice said gently.

Violet nodded.

Beatrice mouth firmed, and she moved the tray to the side, pulling out a large piece of paper. "Then I will help you. Who are the suspects?"

Violet blinked and then said, "Well, the people who were around him over the holidays."

"Do you know who they are?"

"Certainly his family," Violet stood and paced before Beatrice's desk. "There was a sister named Mrs. Stevens. She's a mouthy old thing."

Beatrice scratched the name down. "Did she inherit anything?"

"Supposedly she got the use of Olly's house while she lives, but she had that before."

Beatrice made a note on the paper and added, "Unless something happened between the siblings that would have made her move out. Having a safe place to stay is worth rather a lot."

Violet nodded. "Mrs. Stevens didn't have children, but Olly did. I can't remember their names, but there were two sons. Each of those had two children with a total of four grandchildren. More great-grandchildren, but they're all in the nursery."

Beatrice wrote question marks for the sons' names.

"The grandchildren, however," Violet said, "the two who belong to the older son are Harold and Charlotte. The two who belong to the youngest son are Joseph and Alexander. I believe only the last remains unshackled."

"Did they inherit anything?" Beatrice asked.

Violet frowned. She really didn't know. "We need to know the contents of the will."

Beatrice paused in her notes as she watched Violet pacing.

"Smith could probably get that for you," Beatrice said, sounding conflicted, "but he would certainly break the law to do so."

Violet wasn't sure she cared since they weren't going to do anything nefarious with the information. She did, however, wonder how she'd feel if she were the victim in the same way. She wouldn't like it in the least. But a man was dead. Only she didn't get to choose when to keep the law and not. Instead, she frowned deeply.

"We should probably ask Jack if he can get the information without breaking the law."

Beatrice made a note on a sheet of paper.

"What do we know about the grandsons?"

"Harold is the older child from the older son, Oliver. I would guess that in the long-term he'll inherit the most of what's left."

"So he'd be the one who benefits the most from Olly's death?" Beatrice asked and then shook her head. "Unless his father is living and if that's so, we don't know how his father would leave the things he inherited."

"It's my understanding that there are just heirlooms and the house. A little money but not enough to materially change anyone's lives."

"That's an assumption," Beatrice pointed out, "based on what people think they know about each other. Either of these sons or their children could have lost their money or their position or be in debt and the rest of the family just doesn't know about it yet."

"Too true," Violet said. "I know nothing about Gerald's finances, and he's my oldest brother. Since he doesn't work, it's based entirely off the estate and the generosity of my father. I only know anything about Tomas and Isolde because I helped Tomas get a handle on his inheritance."

Violet nibbled her thumb as she paced. Joseph and Harold and their wives had been at that scavenger hunt. She didn't know if they had actually participated, but Vi had heard enough rumors of the hunt that he and Jack had left to learn that many of the items on the list had required a level of income that would have been hard for the regular working stiff. They wouldn't have attended, would they, if they couldn't afford it?

"Harold is married and has one daughter. His wife,

Phoebe, is at least part of the reason Jack and I were drawn into things. Phoebe, however, maintains that no one killed Olly Rees."

"What if they didn't?" Beatrice asked. "What if it was the paranoid fantasy of whoever left you that note?"

"Then we'll just be wasting our time, I suppose."

CHAPTER 9

When they were finished going over the list of family members they knew about, the list read as follows:

Murder of Olly Rees

SUSPECTS:

Mrs. Stevens — Olly's sister. Was in attendance at the holidays and lives in Olly's house. Confessed to learning more about Violet and brought up the death of Aunt Agatha.

Mr. X Rees— Olly's oldest son. Believed to have been in attendance at the holidays. Primary inheritor? Doesn't seem to have needed Olly's house. Father of Harold and missionary sister.

Mr. X Rees— Olly's other son. Believed to have been in attendance at the holidays. Did he inherit anything? Does he need money? Father of Joseph and other sibling.

Harold Rees— Olly's grandson. Seems to have been a

big fan of his grandfather and upset when it was suggested that Olly was murdered. Was he upset because Olly was murdered? Or was he upset because the secret was out? Did he benefit from his grandfather's death?

Phoebe Rees— Olly's granddaughter-in-law. Seems to have liked him fine. No obvious reason for her to kill her grandfather-in-law. She and Harold seem to be doing fine financially from the outside. Are they really? Called her husband a snake in the grass. Was that because she was drunk or does she know something that others don't?

Joseph Rees— Olly's grandson by the second son. Other than an heirloom surely he wouldn't be the primary inheritor. Seemed quite upset by the idea that Olly may have been murdered.

Delilah Rees— Olly's granddaughter-in-law. Why would she kill Olly?

Charlotte Rees — the Missionary Sister —Olly's granddaughter. At home during the holidays when she often was out of the country. Did she benefit from her grandfather's death? Was it enough to push a supposedly religious woman to such a terrible crime?

Alexander Rees — Joseph's sibling. Single, childless. Seemed exhausted by the antics of Delilah and Phoebe.

Mr. Baldwin. Olly's friend also friends with the earl. Believes Olly was killed as well. Is his saying so a ruse? A way to hide what he did? What possible reason could the man have for murdering his friend?

Who else was there?

QUESTIONS —

1. What was in the will?
2. Is Phoebe right that there wasn't enough money from Olly for anyone to murder him?
3. What are the finances like for the members of the Rees family? Is anyone in dire straits?
4. Maybe it isn't about money. Maybe it was about a family secret?
5. Did Olly know something that would have ruined someone's life? Is there a way to find out now that he's dead?
6. Did a doctor look at Olly's body after he died? If so, did they just assume he passed away? How was Olly found? Will the doctor talk to anyone? Perhaps Jack?

Violet and Beatrice looked over the large paper. Together they leaned back and lifted their cups, taking sanctuary in their hot drinks.

"This always makes me feel a little dirty," Beatrice said. "Like I'm wading through the muck of someone else's life."

"You are," Violet agreed. "We are. We did. We're prying into the muck and writing it on our papers or chalkboards and dissecting their lives and it's not a very a kind thing to do, really."

Beatrice freshened their cups, hers of tea and Violet's with coffee, and they both shuddered a little as they looked the list over.

"It never covers everything," Violet said. "It doesn't cover how Delilah is baby hungry and married for who knows how long. Months and months of realizing when the fateful day comes that yet again she isn't with child. Or watching Phoebe grow with a baby that she'd just as soon not have."

Beatrice winced. "That would be painful. Extraordinarily so, I would imagine."

Violet nodded, thinking about all the women in her life pregnant or already with a child. "It doesn't take into account the days Olly spent with his grandchildren and the love they have for him. Some of them, at least, would never consider hurting their grandfather. The very idea would be abhorrent to them."

"These are all the surface level things we can see from the outside. When I see this, I don't see a murder. I see a normal family. I guess it is necessary to delve a little deeper."

"We need to know more," Violet agreed. "We need to know if anyone was hurting financially. Who benefited from the death. If they have skeletons in their closet. And if so what those skeletons are."

Beatrice looked the paper over again. "Or you could not. You may be invited to this house party, but you don't have to go. You could take what you've learned to an investigator and give him the information and excuse yourself. You don't have an obligation here, Vi."

Violet sipped her coffee and realized that she knew she didn't have to. She had no obligation like they'd pointed out time and again, but she was also sure she wouldn't be walking away from this. She and Jack might not find out what happened to Olly Rees, but Violet wanted at least to try. To know she had done her best before she left it behind her.

Violet finished her coffee and scone with Beatrice

and left the woman to her work while Violet went to hunt down Jack. She wasn't surprised to find him with Smith.

She tossed them both the paper she and Beatrice had made.

"We had another visitor," Jack told Violet as she curled into a chair near the fire. He and Smith were conversing near the desk in the library and Violet had thought to read and let her mind wander about the case, picking at the threads.

"All right?" Violet said, glancing between the two of them.

"An anonymous visitor who left things in the mail slot," Jack said.

"Why is this person being anonymous?" Violet demanded. "Did they run away again?"

"I have no idea. It isn't even helpful." Jack picked up an envelope and tossed it to the side. "Smith thinks whoever is doing this knows for certain that Olly has been murdered. He says any reasonable person would fall into line and believe that the grandfather just passed away."

Violet hadn't thought of that. "Really?"

Smith held out his hands. "Well, yes. Normal people don't see a dead person and think 'murder.' That's particular to Yard men, me, and you, Vi. If Beatrice found her grandfather dead in his bed, she'd start making comments about the full life he had led and how much he'd be missed. She wouldn't be looking for the location of the pillow or whether it looked like there had been a struggle."

Violet leaned back in a bit of a horror. "You know…I

hate that. I hate that the way I think has changed so much."

"It's changed to what is, Vi," Smith said while Jack watched them. "You've stepped out from the herd and among the wolves."

Violet frowned at him. "I don't care how you categorize the whole of mankind, but Beatrice better not be another sheep in your mind."

"She's not a sheep," Smith said idly, entirely unperturbed by Violet's injunction. "She's both better than the sheep and the wolves, particular unto herself."

Violet frowned as she stared at Smith's angelic face. He seemed in earnest, but Beatrice was important to Vi. "If you persuade her to hand over her heart, you had better take care of it."

"A wolf doesn't change it stripes, Vi," Smith said, but there was an edge of dare to him.

"But they do mate for life," Violet shot back, ignoring his mixed metaphor. "And, she knows what you are. I know what you are. No one is unaware of that, Smith. Be a wolf. Just be a wolf who is good to his mate."

Smith lifted a brow but he didn't argue further. It was worse that way, Violet thought. There were no promises given and no idea what was going on behind those hellishly pretty eyes of his. Violet ground her teeth and then saw the flash of humor in Smith's idle face.

She shook her head and then snapped at Jack, "What did they send? This anonymous fool."

Jack rose and handed her the envelope. "It's a list of who was there for the holidays, which I got from Baldwin, Rees' friend. And a note on how he was found.

Nothing useful. He was found a few days after Christmas in his bed. He didn't come down for breakfast, which was unusual any time of the year and especially unusual with guests in the house. The family eventually went after him to see if he was unwell and needed anything."

"Who did specifically?" Violet asked.

"His second son. The man's name is Edgar Rees. He went up, found Olly, and called for help within minutes of leaving the breakfast room."

"So there wasn't enough time for Edgar to have murdered him?"

"And there is your wolf, Violet." Smith glanced at Jack before he added, "It only takes a few minutes to really smother someone, Vi. Edgar could have killed him. The real question is who touched his body and did they note if it was cold or warm. Warm? Edgar could easily be your man. Cold? We're looking at a middle-of-the night scenario and it could have been anyone in the house."

"Was he smothered?"

Jack shifted and then answered almost unwillingly. "That's our best guess. There was no sign of illness. It's possible it was poison but we're not talking about brilliant criminals here. This was the act of a desperate person who was working with what they had on hand. A pillow over the face of an old man who is sleeping is pretty obvious."

Violet skimmed the letter, shook her head at its general uselessness and then noted the invitation. She pulled it from the envelope and found that they had, after all, been invited to a house party to be held by Macie Stevens. Given that her brother had died in that house less than a month before, it was shocking to say the least to invite guests over for the weekend. Violet could only imagine she intended to get away with it by fixing on her crotchety old woman crown.

"Are we going?" Jack asked.

"Yes," Violet said, instantly.

"Take Beatrice as your maid again," Smith said. "I'll be about."

"Perhaps Beatrice has her own things to do," Violet suggested.

Smith laughed low. "You realize, of course, that she'll do whatever you want, Lady Violet." He stressed her title with a mean sarcasm.

"Beatrice loves Violet because Violet took her from being a housemaid to allowing her to be her own woman," Jack shot out. "Don't take it out on Violet that the woman you care for cares about more than just your opinion."

"Beatrice, as a maid, can get gossip out of the servants," Smith returned. "She's lovely, clever, kind, and personable. They'll talk to her when they'd never talk to you or the police. Beatrice may well crack this case while you two are diving into cocktails with the idiots in this family."

Violet lifted a brow, waiting to see if Smith was going to spit out anything else.

"And yes, I know why Beatrice likes and respects Violet. To be honest, it's why I like and respect Violet. You have my loyalty, whatever it's worth, Lady Vi—" For the first time her name didn't feel like an insult, "— because you recognized Beatrice and helped her. Beatrice, Ginny, who else? Me even?" He laughed mockingly and added sarcastically, "That's going too far, I think. We can't expect that level of miracle from even one such as you, Violet."

Before Violet could answer, he rose and faded from the library, leaving Violet and Jack gaping at each other.

CHAPTER 10

*V*iolet faced her closet and then glanced back at Jack.

"We don't have to," he repeated. He'd said so several times already.

"Have you noticed my megrims are gone?"

He nodded slowly, almost unwillingly. Violet laughed and then darted across the room to jump into his arms. He caught her, leaving her hands free to hold his face between her palms. She placed a kiss on his lips, soft and sweet and then leaned back.

"If being nosy, interfering house guests keeps me out of the grey days, Jack, I will dive into this problem, which is none of my concern. Then, take all the spare moments to enjoy how good it is to feel my unfettered love for you without all of the issues of my head and heart getting in the way."

Jack replied with a fervent kiss that left her breathless and delayed their packing for some time. They ended up with another casual evening, a picnic in their bedroom while they slowly worked through packing their bags for the weekend. Violet felt as though they were rebelling against the manners and traditions they'd be succumbing to in a traditional house party. They put a blanket on the floor and ate cheese, crackers, cold meats, and had ginger wine for Vi and port for Jack.

When they finished, Violet brushed off her kimono and then returned to her closet. Three evenings at the house, so she packed the first three evening dresses she found. A blush pink dress with an overlay of black lace that reached her calves, dipped low in the back, high around her neck, and set off her new chandelier earbobs from Jack. Violet popped those in her jewelry box and added her long strand of cream-colored pearls. Matching shoes and headpieces, undergarments, and Violet turned to the next dress.

This one was navy blue, fringed from shoulder to hem and shot through with silver threading. To that dress, Violet packed her matching headpiece, shoes, and then turned to her jewelry. Jack had gotten her sapphire earbobs for Christmas, and Aunt Agatha had left her a diamond and sapphire choker with matching bracelets. She decided she'd layer her favorite bangles and pearls along with them.

The last dress was the brilliantly deep purple that Violet thought of as royal purple. It seemed at first to be the simplest of the dresses, but embroidery of the same hue with a few strands of lavender and silver thread covered every inch of the dress. It was elegant and beautiful and quite unusual to the dresses of the day. Violet, however, loved the dress against her naturally creamy skin, dark hair, and dark eyes.

She glanced through her packed jewelry and decided a mix of what she'd already set aside would do for this dress. Violet added the necessaries and then took out several day dresses, an alternative dress just in case something untoward occurred, and added her favorite pajamas and kimono.

"Is that everything?" she asked Jack. "I feel always as if I'm forgetting something obvious that I'll miss while we're gone."

"When we're not nosing through all their secrets, you might want a book or two."

Violet's condescending glance had him holding up his hands in surrender. She pulled the bag she intended to bring with her in the auto and added her journal, the book she was reading along with the one she intended to read next, her favorite pen in its case. She put her jewelry into that bag and cosmetics and a few other sundries.

Violet threw herself on her bed when she'd finished. "I wonder who else is going to this? Will it be a family party with us as the awkward extras or will Mrs. Stevens cushion the oddness?"

Jack shook his head. "It's why we're bringing our auto. The moment we're done, murderer found or not, we're going to leave."

Violet grinned at him. "You have your knight in armor persona gleaming. All protective and careful."

"Quiet," Jack said with a laugh.

"It's not your fault you're so heroic, darling," Violet teased. "It's just how you are."

Jack placed his hand gently over her mouth. "I'm

going to visit with the earl's friend again in the morning, if I can find him at the club. I'd like to get his take on that list of yours. Given that I won't be able to investigate in my usual manner, I feel a bit like I'm following in your footsteps rather than setting my pace."

Violet choked on a laugh. "I'll lead you along, darling. First, you'll need to casually bring up people's secrets in front of them. And look for chances to gossip."

Jack's brows lifted and he tried to huff. "Men don't gossip. That's a woman's purview."

"Right, of course," Violet mocked. "Like when Father had already heard about the odd surroundings of Olly Rees' death because he and his friend were just exchanging information in a military fashion rather than gossiping over port and cigars."

Jack groaned.

"Gossips. The lot of you men."

"No, no, you don't understand. It's the problem of the limited nature of women's minds."

Violet gasped and leapt for his back but he expected it, and he turned to grab her in his arms instead. He lifted her high and then pressed a kiss on her forehead.

"No kisses for you, sirrah!" she declared. "Limited nature! That's in the man's mind."

"Foolish men," he agreed, "who assume that women aren't as capable themselves and then are incessantly surprised by the things the women in their lives accomplish."

Violet's head tilted as she examined his face and then she leaned forward to whisper in his ear. Her words had his fingers digging into her spine and then he kissed her once again. "You are everything for me, Vi. Without you, I fear I would be nothing more than a husk."

THE HOUSE WAS NICE ENOUGH. It was large without being sprawling. The guests would be housed rather tightly, however. It seemed that there had been rather more acreage in the past, but things had changed and the family wasn't quite as wealthy as it had once been. Houses could be seen in the distance, chimneys with puffs of smoke above them. The scent of fresh country air mixed with the scent of oil from the autos that were left along the drive.

Jack stopped the auto and then got out to hand Violet and Beatrice from the auto. Beatrice was in the plainest of her dresses and had set aside the small upgrades she'd made to her wardrobe over the years of promotions to look the part of a proper lady's maid.

She approached the waiting servant who helped her with the luggage while Jack and Violet approached the front doors. A servant opened the doors before they could knock. The woman wore a black and white dress with a starched apron and greeted them formally as they entered.

"Hullo, hullo," Violet said merrily as they were shown into the parlor, her hand gripping Jack's forearm rather tightly.

The gentlemen rose while Phoebe waved rather lack-adaisically from the sofa. "I didn't think you'd come." Phoebe glanced around to take in everyone else's reactions before she added, "Why would you?"

"Boredom," Violet answered merrily. "Out and out winter blues. Is your daughter here?"

"Up in the nursery," Phoebe said without enthusiasm. She glanced around the room, ignoring the sofa filled with the older ladies, the gents who were talking in a circle near the fire, the servant who was hovering helpfully. There was another younger woman across the room in the chair next to the older women. Given her conservative dress and the looks similar to the Rees men, Violet assumed she was seeing the missionary sister, Charlotte. "I'm sure she'll be about, but we'll keep her from being underfoot. Don't worry."

"Perhaps Violet likes children," Delilah said acidly.

"No one really likes anyone else's children," Phoebe countered. "Only a mother could love those sticky, smelly creatures."

Violet winced for both of them as they shot daggered glances at each other. There was no love lost between those two. Violet could only imagine that with enough time of watching Phoebe not appreciate her child, Delilah had developed a well and truly horrific fury.

"I do enjoy little ones," Violet said firmly. "Though, perhaps, I have a preference for my brother's children."

"Did the heir finally marry?" Mrs. Stevens asked. "I assumed that he never would at this point."

"He's not that old," Violet defended. She was done rolling for this woman simply because she was old. "He is engaged to be married. I was referring to my twin, Victor. He has twin daughters who are only a few months old."

"Does he?" Delilah asked. "Twin daughters sound like

such a miracle. Do they look the same? Do you have a photograph?"

"They do," Violet said. "It is, however, possible to tell them apart if you know them. And yes, I even have it with me, and I'll find it and show them to you."

"Do you know them, though?" Phoebe demanded. "Surely you don't spend all that much time with them."

"Every second I can," Violet said unequivocally. "I adore their perfect little selves."

"Are you unable to have children? Is that why you're obsessed with your brother's children?" Phoebe was the one who asked, and the question was mean, but Delilah was the one who flinched.

"My twin brother's daughters might as well be my own," Violet snapped back. "Whether I have a dozen of my own, I will adore my twin's. And am I obsessed? Yes. Completely."

Phoebe snorted, but Violet's face didn't soften in the least. The gents had, thankfully, gathered near the fire, so Jack wasn't stiffening with fury while Violet, Phoebe, and Delilah argued in their politest voices.

"Perhaps it's a twin thing," Phoebe condescended. "I can't imagine that it would be anything else."

"You're projecting your own dislike of having children onto everyone else," Delilah hissed. "You should be counting your blessings for Alice."

"I don't dislike having children," Phoebe said idly. "I dislike being pregnant. Given I would be happy with just my sweetling, I don't see why I must have child after child to continue an ancestral line that no one else cares about. It isn't like there's a title to carry on. It isn't like there's an estate to hand down. Father Oliver works.

Harold works. Our child will work. There is no need to preserve the family name that no one cares about but us."

"You don't care about continuing the family name?" Delilah asked aghast.

"Obviously not," Phoebe said dismissively. "I suppose I'd be more interested in having child after child if I was. Violet understands. Her husband doesn't have a grand family estate to carry on either. One child, male or female, and she'll be done."

"Oh, I want more children than that," Violet said, done with the conversation. "Funny weather we're having. Don't you think so, Delilah?"

Delilah agreed and then said something about the long streak of rainy days leaving her hair frizzy. "And it's so cold."

"Indeed," Violet said. "Quite reaches into your bones, doesn't it?"

"Your rooms will be ready soon," Delilah said. "The housekeepers are a bit behind. The daily help that comes in isn't really enough for a party so large."

"Of course." Violet looked around the room, noting the two cousins standing side-by-side with their fathers, another old gent, and—oh! It couldn't be. Violet leaned forward. It was. Vi closed her eyes and breathed slowly in through her nose, striving for patience. Jack stood directly next to the old gent and the next person over was none other than Miss Emily Allen, Jack's one-time fiancé and a reporter. What madness was this and just how did they end up at the same house party?"

Violet met Jack's gaze and his was full of apology. She knew he'd had no idea. He would have warned her and let her decide whether they were going to come after all.

Vi smiled at him, full of a promise that she wasn't mad and he relaxed under her gentle nod. She didn't hold him accountable for having once loved the woman. It was just…not what Violet needed or wanted. She winked at him, but he wasn't so easily dissuaded from reality. Whether they liked it or not, Emily Allen was once again in their eyes and her gaze was far too observant for anyone's good.

CHAPTER 11

"Why is she here?" Violet hissed as she glanced through the bedroom. Beatrice, the perfect maid, had already unpacked all of Violet's clothes and seen them steamed from their wrinkles. Her gown for that evening—the purple one—was hanging on the side of the mirror with Violet's accessories. "Oh, I missed her as a maid. Look at my dresses! Perfection."

"Don't get used to it," Smith said, and Violet choked on a scream. "Are you talking about Miss Allen? I read her articles about you. They were my favorite reading of the last year."

Jack roughly grabbed Smith's arm. "What do you think you're doing?"

"I'm the help man. Just here to light the fires."

"I've got the fire," Jack growled. "Get out of our rooms."

Smith shrugged. "I've been through everyone else's rooms today. I am also here to report, O Captain, my

Captain." The sarcasm was not the way to calm Jack down.

He growled again and Violet put her hand on his arm. "Smith won't come into our room again." She shot him a commanding look that promised retribution. Unlike Jack who'd get physical, Violet would just pull in Beatrice. "And you'll calm down," she said to Jack.

Jack let go of Smith and then stepped back. His jaw was still tight, and he was still tense, but he'd calmed down enough to not murder Smith.

Violet turned to Smith, who held the same smirk as usual. From his expression, it was like nothing had happened even though Smith hadn't been able to get free. Or at least get free without causing things to escalate further.

Vi kept herself from shaking her finger at the two of them and then scolding them like schoolboys. Her gaze narrowed on Smith. "If you scare me like that again, I'll tell Beatrice."

He lifted a brow and his smile was mocking, but Violet was guessing that her threat would work better than he'd like.

To Jack, she said, "We need to learn what he's found out."

"He's going to get shot if he isn't careful. Slipping in and out of people's rooms will get a man killed." Jack's fury was barely restrained and she took hold of his hand to be sure he'd hesitate before he lashed out.

"Jack," Violet said gently, "Smith knows that. He's well aware of the risks. He's a wolf, just like us."

Smith snorted. "I should have been careful when it came to your rooms." Vi about died when he explained. "I didn't want to be caught entering them. I am supposed to be preparing the dining room." He laughed. "I suspect I may be let go before this weekend is over even though I am temporary help. Or Beatrice will cover for me."

"She's probably covering for you right now," Violet agreed. "What did you find out?"

"Joseph keeps a journal. He's not in any financial trouble. His biggest woe is that his wife can't get pregnant, and he's sure it's his fault. Something about the mumps and failing her. It's all very dramatic for a bloke. I blush for him."

Violet waited as Jack finally sat down on the end of the bed and tugged her to join him. "Ahhh," Violet said. "He looked after drunk Phoebe and worries over his wife's happiness and their children."

Smith snorted. "He doesn't want to adopt even though she does, and he thinks she's gained too much weight and needs to be less rude to Phoebe who is 'a good gal.'"

"Phoebe is a vicious snake when it comes to Delilah." Violet stretched her arms back and glanced at the clock. "We're supposed to be ready soon for dinner. What else do you know?"

Smith spread his hands. "Nothing really. Phoebe and Harold weren't helpful enough to leave out a handy journal or letters. I tried for the library and the will, but I haven't been able to get access yet. The old woman was in her rooms and then her maid was in there. I'll have to try during dinner for the Stevens woman's room."

Violet nodded. "Go then. We need to dress. The will would be incredibly helpful. Or letters between the family members. Olly Rees would likely have kept them. People of his generation often do."

Smith shot Violet a look that said she was telling an expert what to do.

"Fine, apologies," Violet said to Smith. "Out."

"Look through Olly Rees' room," Jack said. "He might well keep private papers in his bedroom."

Smith's glance to Jack said the same thing that his look to Violet had said. Don't tell him how to do this. He was better, Violet thought, at breaking the rules.

Violet took a long breath in and then walked to the bathroom. The door was locked and as she returned to their bedroom, she had a moment of feeling entirely put out not to have a private bath. She glanced at Jack, who read her face and then laughed. Violet crossed to the dress and examined it. They'd spent several hours in the auto and she wanted to at least rinse her body before she dressed. She frowned at the bath door and then crossed and knocked.

"One moment," a female's voice called, and Violet had no idea if it was Phoebe, Delilah, or the sister, Charlotte.

"Thank you," Violet replied and went back to the room to find Jack shaving, using the pitcher and bowl in the room that Beatrice had filled if Violet had to guess.

"It felt like Phoebe was deliberately trying to upset Delilah," Violet told him, watching him shave. "It felt like an attack and she was using me to do so, which I didn't like at all."

Jack lifted his brows. "Why aren't you talking about the other thing?"

"You mean Miss Allen?"

Jack's expression told Violet that he didn't want to play games.

"Jack," Violet said gently. "I know that you love me. We're long past the moment when I met her and had no idea that you were once engaged to her."

Jack winced at the reminder. "Ah, the good old days."

Violet chuckled. She didn't like Emily Allen, but she wasn't afraid of the woman coming between her and Jack.

"I had a moment of fear that you'd throw me over in a fury when you met her," Jack confessed.

"But I didn't." Violet patted his cheek and then pushed up on her toes to kiss his chin. "I love you, Jack. We should have guessed that Miss Allen would be invited given that Mrs. Stevens said she had talked to her about us. It's so odd that they're having this house party in the same house where the man died so recently."

"It is in poor taste," Jack agreed and then winked as he added, "as is our being here."

"At least we didn't know Mr. Rees. Most of these people are thinking about the last time they were here. He was here, he was the host, and that was just weeks ago. That's in far more poor taste than us being here."

"Oh yes," Jack said sarcastically, "Their having greater poor taste absolutely alleviates ours."

Violet snorted even though they both believed that just because one person stole jewelry and the other person stole a coat, they were both thieves. One person's greater crime didn't change the crime the other person committed.

Violet checked the bath and found it empty. She left Jack behind, rinsing herself, washing her face, and freshening her hair before she turned to the bedroom where she put on her dress, stockings, and then turned to her cosmetics and jewelry. When she finished dressing, she took Jack's arm and asked, "What shall we do? Just watch?"

"I think we should nudge," Jack said. "Up the problem and try to draw out the drama. We need information."

Violet paused, immediately balking to do as Jack suggested and then agreeing it was the best. They didn't have long to solve this possible murder. Better to spur the family into a fight and hope they'd let some tidbits drop.

The house wasn't so large to get lost and they found others in the hallway as they made their way down the stairs. Violet introduced herself to the woman who had the room next to theirs and found herself talking to Charlotte, Harold's sister.

"I'm sorry," Charlotte said after she trailed off for the third time. "I'm just a little uncomfortable with this whole thing. I think Aunt Stevens should not be having this party right now."

"Were you close with Mr. Rees?" Violet asked.

Charlotte paused and then explained, "As a child, yes. Father didn't live so far from here, and Grandmother wanted us around as often as possible. I married a missionary, you know. My dear husband and I live in the Territory of New Guinea."

"Where is that? Is it in the Caribbean?"

Charlotte shook her head. "It's an island in Australia."

"Oh is it? It's quite hot there, isn't it?"

"It's summer in Australia right now," Charlotte

agreed. "It's rather nice to avoid the worst of the heat there with a little home-flavored rain."

"So you haven't been as close to your grandfather since spending so much time away?"

Charlotte nodded and then paused to hold her fingers to her mouth. "I knew I would lose time with him," she said with a shaking voice. "But I didn't realize how hard it would be when the chance to change my mind had passed. Perhaps we could have done better work closer to home. Perhaps our relationships and kindnesses here, in our own vineyard so to speak, was what we should have done. It has sent my husband and I for quite a loop."

Violet gasped. "Are you thinking of staying in England?"

"It's bad enough, isn't it? With Grandfather? What will it be like when it's Father? It's not just my father, of course. Liam is thinking the same thing with his parents and grandparents. He's lucky enough to still have all of them. Why should we toss that bounty away?"

Violet paused and then admitted, "I couldn't leave my family. Not for years. You were brave to do so, but perhaps it is time to come home."

Charlotte sniffed and then glanced back. "I do wish Liam would hurry along. Vanity is his worst trait." She laughed low and then was teary again when she said, "Grandfather did love to tease him about it. Every time he sent Liam a gift, it was some sort of pomade, a comb, a little pair of scissors. Oh! Listen to me. Listen to me weeping on your shoulder. How do you know my grandfather?"

Violet hated herself for fudging but she said, "Your Grandfather and great aunt and my family have known each other for quite some time. Did you know that your aunt knew my grandmother and mother better than I did? Such an odd world when you think about it."

"Have you lost both your grandmother and mother?"

Violet nodded. "I believe Oscar Wilde would describe me as quite negligent."

Charlotte paused and then surprised herself and Violet with a watery laugh. "Negligent indeed. Both of us. Losing our family as we have." She smiled at Violet and reached out to take her hand and squeeze it. "Thank you. I needed that. And perhaps to see someone who has made it through the worst of the mourning."

CHAPTER 12

*T*he dining hall was full. Mrs. Stevens sat at the head of the table with Miss Allen, Mr. Baldwin—the earl's friend—the children and grandchildren of Olly Rees all in attendance, leaving Jack and Violet as the only ones unfamiliar with the family. While Violet wasn't concerned about Emily Allen's effect on Jack, she was relieved when they were seated at opposite ends of the table.

The guests ate quietly with uncomfortable glances around that declared they all knew they shouldn't be there. Neither Violet nor Jack tried to press for information. It was simply too awkward and in bad taste given the level of discomfort. Conversations started and then faded into nothing, other than a rather long and tedious discussion between Joseph and Mr. Baldwin on the effect of chills on old wounds.

Once that conversation petered out, everyone returned to staring at their plates until Mrs. Stevens

stood. She ignored every dark look cast her way as she
lifted her glass.

"To my brother," Mrs. Stevens said, looking around
the table. "Strong, energetic, aware, precise, and quite
young for our family to be dead. The youngest, in fact,
for four generations other than those who died in war,
childbirth, and a rather idiotic hot air balloon accident."

Phoebe choked on her wine as Mrs. Stevens tilted her
head and looked around the table.

"Look at you all. Lying to yourselves. Telling yourself
that poor Olly succumbed quietly to death's embrace.
Dying in his sleep for no reason whatsoever."

Those around the table started mumbling a low roar
of whispering. Olly's sons were staring at their aunt in
horror while Delilah had started to weep, drawing a
scowl from Phoebe, who seemed offended by Delilah's
tears. The sons of Olly Rees and their wives were stoic,
but their gazes were hard.

"He wasn't ill, was he?" Mrs. Stevens asked.

No one answered.

"Was he?" she demanded more stridently.

Again, no one answered but several shuffled in their
seats.

"He didn't even have a sniffle, did he, Joseph?"

Joseph gasped at his name and his weeping wife
reached over and took his hand as he stammered.
"Grandfather Olly seemed quite well before he died,
Aunt Stevens, but—"

"No buts," Mrs. Stevens said sharply, cutting Joseph
off. "He wasn't ill. He wasn't struggling with his heart.
Did you know he'd just been to the doctor? Alexander
did you know that?"

To Violet's surprise, Alexander nodded.

No one else answered.

Mrs. Stevens seemed to loom even higher over the table, glancing down at each of her relatives. "You each have grasped onto the idea that Olly succumbed in his sleep despite Dr. Welch having said he was quite healthy only weeks before. Dear Olly's heart was strong, his lungs were clear, he had no inexplicable pain."

"It could have been an apoplectic fit," Delilah said. "A friend of my father's collapsed suddenly just months ago."

Violet winced when Mrs. Stevens fiery gaze turned on Delilah.

"There were signs of struggle weren't there, Edgar?" Mrs. Stevens demanded without looking away from Delilah.

Olly's second son hesitated but weakened when his aunt's gaze darted to him. "I suppose he could have been quite uncomfortable when he passed."

"Or he could have been smothered," Mrs. Stevens snapped. "You know he slept like the dead, never moving. That wasn't what the room looked like – someone could have held a pillow over my dear brother's face and stolen his life."

"Aunt Stevens," Oliver, the older of Olly's sons said, "that is quite enough of that."

"Do you think I don't know what you're doing, Oliver? Edgar? I think you realized that something unto-ward happened to your father and you realized that one of your children could have been responsible. Was likely responsible—"

Charlotte gasped, glancing about the table as though

she couldn't imagine such a terrible thing. But, Violet thought, she might well have been entirely unaware of what had been happening among the family. They surely would have been out of the habit of including the distant, solitary granddaughter of Olly Rees.

The table's murmuring was rabid, but Charlotte's voice cut through it with a high-pitched demand. "Why would anyone have killed Grandfather? He didn't have enemies. Did he?"

Again, no one answered.

"Did he?" Charlotte almost screeched.

"Of course he didn't, Lottie," her father assured her. "Aunt Stevens, let's calm down now, shall we? This is all quite dramatic."

Mrs. Stevens snorted.

Charlotte's husband wrapped an arm around her shoulders. "It is possible that he passed away in his sleep. You might be a long-lived family, but to expect that you will all be so blessed is a special sort of arrogance."

Mrs. Stevens laughed coldly. "It is also a special sort of arrogance to see only what you want to see rather than what is before you."

"But is it before us?" Edgar asked, remaining calm. He glanced towards his two sons and their wives and then back to his aunt. "I have never seen anything more horrible than my father lying dead when I expected to find him having a lie-in with a good book."

Violet reached under the table and took Jack's hand as the family turned on each other. It was the pained looks on their faces that truly upset Vi. This was a family who was overall nauseated by the sheer idea that someone had stolen their grandfather. The cousins Joseph and

Harold were both holding their wives while Joseph also had a hand on Harold's shoulder. Delilah was weeping while Charlotte was a sickly pale.

The two sons of Olly were both white. Their wives were silent, but each had signs of stress. Mrs. Edgar's wife was holding a clenched handkerchief between her fingers while Mrs. Oliver Rees was pale, but her attention was on her husband. Violet could see Mrs. Oliver's hand moving as she rubbed her husband's back consolingly.

Mr. Baldwin and Miss Allen were both silent and composed. Did Violet and Jack look the same? Were they as emotionless of observers as the other two while the Rees family fell apart?

"That is enough, Aunt Stevens," Oliver Rees said. He stood as he faced his aunt. "We loved Father. Of course we did. Why would any of us murder him?"

Mrs. Stevens placed her hand on her stomach as if she were ill. "That's why I'm so confused." Her mouth trembled. "We aren't perfect, but we aren't a bad family. Olly was always so proud of how close we have been. By how much the children loved each other. By how much we knew and cared for each other. But now...my goodness, what has happened? Why, why did someone kill my brother?"

Before anyone could answer, Mrs. Stevens hurried from the dining room. The clatter of her heels down the hall, up the stairs, and the slamming of doors was followed by silence.

"Oh my," Mrs. Oliver Rees murmured.

Her husband, Oliver, said, "I know it's rather awful. But perhaps we had better adjourn for the evening."

His gaze was fixed on the guests over the family. Mr. Baldwin rose and handed Miss Allen to her feet. He glanced around the room and said carefully, "Regardless of how he died, he loved you all. Being with you was the great joy of his life, and he died a happy man."

The condolences fell flat given that Olly was dead. Surely as he'd died, if he had struggled, he'd woken up and realized that someone was murdering him. Delilah whimpered and then cried into her handkerchief. Jack stood next, and Violet joined him immediately. Jack nodded and then stepped from the room with Violet on his arm. They were silent as they left. Mr. Baldwin and Miss Allen had already disappeared giving them the chance to reach back and almost close the door.

Vi gave Jack a silent squeeze and they both paused for a moment, listening. There was no sound of anyone else shoving away from the table in the dining room and they waited.

"I don't understand," a man said. Violet guessed that was Harold. "Why is everyone so convinced that Grandfather was murdered? It's not like he had some wonderful fortune that was left behind. We're all carrying on as we were before but for missing him."

The reply was only the sniffling of several of the family members. Others had succumbed beyond Delilah and it sounded as if most or all of the women were crying. The fact that the family had drawn together made Violet want to weep herself. She pressed her face against Jack's chest.

Perhaps it wasn't a murder? Perhaps it was something entirely different? Maybe it was just an apoplectic fit? Violet had heard a story of quite a young man dying from one of those. Perhaps Mrs. Stevens didn't want to believe that she'd lost her brother and would spend the rest of her days without her expected companions of husband and brother.

She pulled back, distracted by a preternatural awareness and barely kept in a scream. Her start made Jack glance in the direction she was looking. Smith was mere inches from them. He placed a finger of his lips and jerked his head down the hall.

They followed him since the family was only silently crying and would no doubt leave the table soon. There was nothing more to learn there. Smith led them through halls they had not seen and into the library. Beatrice was standing just behind the door. He locked the side entrance behind them and then silently crossed the floor, locking the main entrance.

"We'll have to be quick if someone comes to the door," Smith said. "But after all of that overwrought emotion, I think we'll be safe."

"It is not overwrought emotion," Beatrice hissed, "when you are grieving someone who was a right old gent and a good man. It's what he deserves."

Smith didn't argue. He crossed to the desk and opened a drawer. Inside was an account book along with the will. They were just there in the top drawer as though they would be nowhere else.

"It's like they have nothing to hide," Violet said low.

"They don't," Beatrice said. "I made a good few enemies today trying to ferret out secrets. Mr. Olly Rees was a good master, a good man, and a good grandfather, father, and brother. He seems to have been a saint."

"No one is a saint," Jack said flatly.

"Agreed," Smith said, nodding once at Jack and then lighting a cigarette. "Everyone has done something that makes them ashamed. Everyone has a day where they lash out at their friends. Or makes a mistake and has to apologize."

Beatrice elbowed Smith and muttered, "I didn't say he was perfect. I said he was a right old gent. I think we'd all have liked him."

Violet rubbed her brow and asked, "Did you read these?"

Smith nodded.

Violet glanced at Beatrice who nodded as well.

"Nothing overtly off?" Vi asked.

"It's all very reasonable," Smith said. "The accounts are all right. There isn't a mass of money, but what there is split between the two sons with the greater portion going to the eldest. The house is in the care of the sister. The grandchildren all received a nice bequest, but it wasn't enough to do anything more than have a good holiday."

"There was nothing at all?" Vi demanded, pressing her fingers against her temple. All of the emotion and tension had left her with a powerful headache.

"The only thing I found was the beginnings of a letter," Smith said. "It was started the night Mr. Rees died and was entirely unfinished."

"Who was it addressed to?" Jack asked.

"Joseph."

Violet frowned. She was back to rubbing her brow as she wondered if that meant anything at all.

Jack groaned. "That's useless."

"I know," Smith muttered.

"I talked to Mr. Rees' man. He cleaned up the bedroom after Mr. Rees died," Beatrice said quietly. "He was the only servant who didn't seem to mind my questions."

"And," Violet asked.

"He, too, thinks Mr. Rees was murdered."

CHAPTER 13

"*L*et's go back to our bedroom," Jack said, "and assess what we know."

Jack gathered the will and the accounts. He followed by going through the desk and pulling everything that looked like private papers. There was no remorse on his face when he took them and the only one who seemed surprised by it was Beatrice, who said nothing.

"You don't have to be part of this," Violet told Beatrice.

She paused, staring between them and then down at the paperwork before she tidied the stack nervously. "I want to help find the killer too."

Smith's cold smile was chilling as he looked with unmasked approval at Beatrice. Violet glanced at Jack, but he only shook his head. It was like she had said before, Violet thought, Beatrice's choices were her own to make and Violet's job was to be a friend and advise if

Beatrice wanted help. Violet wasn't even sure what she'd say if she were asked for advice. Perhaps something like 'I can understand why you have feelings for him, but his personality is so big and his morals so ambiguous that I'm worried you'll lose yourself.'

Instead, Violet took the paperwork from Beatrice.

"No," Vi said quietly.

Beatrice opened her mouth to protest, but Vi shook her head, regretting the motion when her headache flared.

"If you were found with these, the family could charge you with theft, or worse," Violet told Smith and Beatrice. "They can't really hurt Jack and me. I need you to eavesdrop on the most suspicious of those who leave the dining room and see if you can find out what they truly believe. Bea, in your servant's garb, you can probably linger outside of a bedroom with a tray and listen. Smith, we all know that you probably can crawl up the side of the building and hear with some sort of preternatural ability."

He snorted.

"I will dig through this because if they notice it's gone, well, this is why I was invited even if Macie Stevens isn't saying so."

Violet turned to Jack and what she said next surprised even her. "Talk to Emily. She must know something. We'll meet back in our rooms after the house is quiet and we'll compare notes."

Jack's shock was palpable as Violet pushed up on her toes and kissed his cheek.

"You aren't jealous?" Smith demanded as if he wanted her to admit the truth.

Violet wasn't shocked when she answered. "No. Not really."

"Liar," Smith said.

Violet fixed her gaze on him, her head still throbbing, and thought a lie would be just the thing. "Did you know that Beatrice was once engaged when she was a girl? Just before I hired her?"

Smith's face was unmoving.

"She loved him like the day was long and when they were over, she cried for weeks over mending my stockings."

Beatrice's squeak didn't pull Smith's gaze from Violet. She had always thought him impassive until she saw the cold fury emanating from him. Jack must have seen it too, for he shifted to be closer to her as if to ward off an attack. Or warn her off continuing.

"She might love you or she might still be deciding on her feelings, but she's in something with you now. Whatever that is, until you are resolved, she won't ever step out on you. Do you know why?"

"She has the rare virtue of being an honorable and trustworthy woman." Smith's tone was completely devoid of emotion, which was more unsettling than if he'd been shouting.

Violet just kept herself from rolling her eyes at him. "Rare? Yes. But honorable and trustworthy? Also yes."

"I—" Beatrice squeaked again. "I...stop, please. Vi—"

Violet offered Beatrice an apologetic look before she added, "If Beatrice were to run across an old love of hers and they were to confer in private, you could be sure that all they would do is confer."

Smith nodded once. His jaw was clenched tight and his angel's eyes burned with an unholy light.

"Because she is Beatrice."

Smith nodded again. Given his expression, Violet knew she'd thrown open the tightly contained box where Smith buried his feelings.

"And Jack is Jack," she finished. "I am not a flighty minx ruled by emotion any more than you are an unfeeling bastard incapable of love."

"I have never been engaged," Beatrice finally ground out.

Smith shot Violet a dark glance, full of terrible promises before he told her lightly, "Touché."

Violet snorted and Jack said with some relief, "We have our orders."

Smith and Beatrice left first, Smith seeming to fade away while Beatrice's straight shoulders curled in on herself and she adjusted into a guise of humble servant, one that no longer quite fit, Violet noticed with pleasure. Violet nodded at Jack and went to slip away herself, but he took her arm.

She looked up at him in question.

"I adore you, Mrs. Wakefield."

"And I you," Violet returned. "Emily Allen is our best bet on the next step, and she's a brilliant woman. You do have excellent taste that way."

Violet kissed his chin. She thought about making some quip, but she really thought it might ruin the mood. Instead she winked at him devilishly and left him behind to run up the stairs towards their room and dump all their stolen paperwork on the bed.

How had they gotten pulled into this? Violet thought

about the anonymous letter and who might have sent it. Someone in that family who had been weeping around the table believed that the grandfather had been murdered with enough fervency to draw Violet in. Anyone with a handful of wits and a history of Violet's involvement in murder cases would have to know that drawing in Violet would draw in Jack. And drawing in Jack was drawing in Scotland Yard.

Violet took a few aspirin with a large glass of water, then read through the pile of documents and found nothing that would indicate Olly had been murdered for money or for an inheritance. Whatever had killed Olly Rees wasn't what had killed Aunt Agatha. Violet breathed easier knowing that.

Looking at Aunt Agatha's family, they were a slew of cousins who could expect to inherit something from the woman who had partially raised them. Her death had been, almost from the first, a clear act of greed. For Olly, however, it was not so clear. He hadn't been murdered for his money. They'd already established that. Violet rose and left a note for Jack and then she found her way to Mrs. Stevens's rooms.

Violet knocked on the door and was allowed inside a moment later. The woman was alone and dressed in a frayed flannel nightgown and wool robe. Her gaze was, however, sharp and calculating when she looked Violet over.

"You're rather unexceptional, you know."

Violet snorted and then said, "Yes, I know. Nothing all that remarkable about me except perhaps the fortune I inherited."

"And the respect that so many people have for your

ability to ferret out secrets. That's the problem here, I think," the old woman said, diving straight into the matter. "I've been thinking about it since he died. Olly didn't have enough money to murder over. He didn't have enemies. He wasn't a monster whose death made the world a better place. He was just a kindly old man who loved his family."

Violet rubbed her hands down her arms. "It's terrifying, isn't it?"

Mrs. Stevens glanced at Violet sharply. "What is?"

"Knowing that someone you love is probably a murderer. That you trust them and they might kill you next."

Mrs. Stevens stared at Violet and then the old woman shuddered, shriveling down into a chair. She nodded like a puppet on a string and then pulled a crumpled handkerchief from the pocket of her robe and dabbed it against her eyes.

"There's a part of me that is terrified I'll be next."

Violet nodded. She could see why Mrs. Stevens would think that. If there seemed to be no reason to kill Olly then there didn't need to be a reason to kill her. It must be an overwhelming load to carry. Grief for her brother and closest companion, worry for her family, fury against his killer, and fear for herself and the others she loved.

"Why do you think your brother was killed?"

Mrs. Stevens shook her head. "I have been asking myself that over and over again."

"But you do believe that he was murdered?"

"When I first went into his room and saw him dead," Mrs. Stevens said, openly weeping now, "I thought that the worst had happened and the worst was that he died. Only later as I relived it over and over did I realize he must have been killed. My brother was a sound sleeper. The kind of man who didn't move at all. It was a joke between us as we were children. Or rather, he terrified me with it. I'd think he died. Sometimes he slept with his eyes open. It was awful. I had nightmares about his pranks on me for years after we were separated and sent to different schools."

Violet could guess what came next. "But that morning was different."

"It was more than merely ruffling his bed. If he'd gotten quite ill you could say that, but it was the second pillow on the floor near his bed that was so disturbing."

"A pillow?" Violet felt suddenly that Mrs. Stevens was wrong and their time had been utterly wasted.

"Yes," Mrs. Stevens said flatly.

"Perhaps he knocked it off," Violet suggested. If that was all the reason Mrs. Stevens had to believe her brother had been murdered, Violet was going to be quite put out. Her disbelief was becoming more and more apparent.

"No, you don't understand. He only slept the way he did—perfectly. He didn't move. He didn't roll. When he woke in the morning, he could flatten his blankets out with one simple tug. He was all about the ritual and the stillness. He did everything the same every single night. He'd crack his window, he'd take the extra pillows from his bed and stack them on the chair in his room. He could tolerate only one pillow under his head."

"And?" Violet prompted, but she was beginning to get an image of why the scene was bothering Mrs. Stevens.

"Perhaps that night he needed two pillows because he wanted to sit up and sleep in bed. He might have been restless."

"But he had a routine for that as well." Mrs. Stevens sighed. "He would make himself a hot cup of milk and he'd write out his thoughts. He said if you could get your thoughts out of your mind, you would be able to sleep fine."

Violet frowned. "So he was upset that night, wasn't he?"

"There was a cup of milk."

"Something he would have gotten for himself?"

Mrs. Stevens nodded. "We only have our housekeeper and a daily maid when it's just family here."

"When he was able to sleep, what did his room look like?"

Mrs. Stevens pressed the handkerchief to her eyes again and it took her a few moments to answer. "His sheets would be military tight and flat on a good night or a bad night. He wouldn't toss and turn. If he was upset, he would have his milk, think about what was bothering him. He'd work it through in his mind on paper and then he'd lay in the same position and turn to a series of meditations until he slipped into sleep."

"Was there nothing in his journal?"

"His journal is missing," Mrs. Stevens stated.

And there it was, the proof Violet needed that it was, truly, murder. A man as precise of Olly Rees would not misplace his journal, not when it was of such value to him.

"When you found him in his bed, which was normally very neat, it was a mess."

Mrs. Stevens nodded. "His bed was a mess, an extra pillow was on the floor next to him—that would have never happened no matter how sleepless he was. Even after his wife's death, when he was struggling to sleep well for weeks, he did the same thing. I know what he did. I was here. I would have hot milk with him when I heard him wake. I would let him talk about her to me, so he didn't have to write in his journal alone."

"What did he do after she died?"

"He missed her so much he wept daily for months. At night it was the worst, but he'd get up and drink his milk and write about her in his journal or talk to me, and then he'd go to bed."

"I toss and turn when I can't sleep," Violet said. "I wish I didn't."

"The very fact of his odd sleeping habits are why I think he was murdered," Mrs. Stevens told her. "Even at the worst of times, my brother would lay down on his single pillow, and cross his fingers over his stomach and remain still until he slept. It was his pattern from a seven-year-old to a seventy-year-old."

"A pillow and a missing journal," Violet said. "The simple mistakes of a killer."

"Exactly," Mrs. Stevens agreed. "Now, which one of my beloveds killed him? Because you're right, they're my family, I love them, and one of them murdered my brother. One of them might murder me or someone else I love next. I don't want to lose anyone else."

Violet shook her head helplessly. She wished she could provide that answer.

CHAPTER 14

"Why did you involve me?" Violet asked the old woman.

"I asked Mr. Baldwin, Olly's oldest friend, what to do. He's known Emily for quite a long time and he suggested we confer with her. It was Emily who said we should draw you and Jack in."

Violet had to admit she was shocked to the core of herself. Emily Allen did not care for Violet. They'd come to an unsteady truce but the truth of the matter was that Miss Allen had once been loved by Jack, she'd thrown him over, and when she was ready to draw him back—she failed. Violet didn't think Jack would have been drawn in again even if they hadn't been in love, but Miss Allen blamed Violet for her failure.

Violet took a deep breath and then asked, "Are you the one who sent the letters to my door?"

Mrs. Stevens nodded. "I was afraid you wouldn't help

if it seemed like the delusions of an old woman. I got a neighborhood boy to help me."

Violet admitted to herself that she might have side-stepped or taken the many points that Jack had made about this not being their problem and let him talk her out of it. Violet sighed, hating that Mrs. Stevens could have been right.

Violet started to leave to explain to meet with Jack and share what they'd both discovered, but at the last moment, she turned back. "Who else knew about Mr. Rees' sleeping habits?"

Mrs. Stevens eyes welled. "Everyone."

"So anyone would have known to take the journal?"

"Olly was vocal about his practices. He almost prose-lytized them. Within the family, to be honest, he did. Any one of us would have known to look for the journal if we wanted to hide something."

Violet paced Mrs. Stevens' bedroom. "Which means that there is something to hide. I thought there must have been. However—" Violet glanced at the family photograph on the wall and then back at Mrs. Stevens.

It was the great aunt who finished the idea. "What terrible secret could any of them have that was worth killing their father or grandfather over? I have no idea."

Violet crossed to the woman and took her hands gently. Despite her sharpness and energy for her age, she was in her seventies. Her hands were spotted with age. Her hair was white and thinner than it must have been in her youth. She was a lovely woman for her age, but she was aged, and her family had murdered her beloved brother.

"I'm sorry," Violet whispered.

"I convinced myself I wouldn't lose him until so much later," Mrs. Stevens whispered back. "I wasn't ready for this. I knew my husband would die first. His health was never very good. But, Olly? Not Olly." Her voice cracked and she was racked with tears. "Not Olly. He was my best friend from my earliest day. My best friend, my best defender, my best—" Whatever Mrs. Stevens intended to say didn't make it past her tear-choked throat. "N-n-n-not Olly. Not Olly."

Violet rubbed her back and held her until her tears faded enough to let Mrs. Stevens speak.

"It doesn't stop hurting, losing someone. I know that you know that, Violet. I want to apologize that I was so callous about your aunt. I suppose I thought it wouldn't hurt as much because it wasn't your mother or your husband."

"She was my mother," Violet told Mrs. Stevens flatly. "In all the ways that mattered, she was my mother. She took over being our primary caregiver after our own mother died."

"Our?" Mrs. Stevens asked, yawning around her question. Violet guessed that sleepless nights and the crying jag had pushed Mrs. Stevens from tired to exhausted.

"My twin and I," Violet said, rising. "You need to sleep. Lay down and remember all the good things about your brother, and we'll do what we can to find his killer and protect your loved ones."

Mrs. Stevens didn't object when Violet helped her to rise and to get her into bed or when Violet took the extra key to the bedroom and locked the door. Violet stared at it for a long time before starting back towards the room she shared with Jack.

"What were you doing in there?" Phoebe demanded.

"Talking to Mrs. Stevens about my aunt." Violet glanced Phoebe over and realized that Phoebe, at least, hadn't been one of the weeping Reeses at the table. She was dry-eyed and seemingly unbothered.

"Why?"

"Because," Violet said quietly. "I know what it feels like to lose."

Phoebe snorted and then stepped back when Violet's gaze narrowed on her. "It didn't sound so bad. Gaining such a fortune."

Violet barely held back an animalistic growl as she hissed, "I was always rich enough. I'd give away every cent I have to get my aunt back. You are foolish if you think money buys happiness."

Phoebe scowled at Violet and muttered, "What do you know about what it's like to be poor?"

"You aren't poor," Violet snapped. "You don't know anything about being poor."

"And you do?" Phoebe shot back.

"Yes," Violet said. "My ward lived in a hovel, doing her best to support her grandmother as a child. I've seen real poverty. You're just not as rich as you'd like to be. There's a difference between not swimming in ready money and being poor, Phoebe."

Phoebe glared at Violet but she just shook her head and left her behind.

"You are a busybody interfering where you aren't wanted," Phoebe called after her. "No one killed Olly and all you're doing is encouraging an old woman in her fantasies."

Violet didn't bother dignifying Phoebe with a

response. She went to the floor were her room was and found Jack, Smith, and Beatrice.

Jack shook his head at Vi, taking her by the back of the neck as he said, "When I didn't find you here…"

Violet let him tug her close even as she murmured, "I left a note."

Jack breathed in deeply and then blew out slowly. "I knew you were all right and I was still worried."

Violet was touched more than she had been in the past. Her fears at losing him made his fears of losing her more understandable, even when his worry was over what she considered nothing. It was fine. He was protective, which was one of the ways he showed his love. "Let me tell you what I learned."

Violet recapped her conversation with Mrs. Stevens and Jack grunted.

"It seems conclusive at this point," Beatrice said. "Not that we didn't think so before, but those are telling details."

Violet nodded. "Someone has a dark skeleton in the closet. We need to find a way to discover who."

"They all seem so normal. Not necessarily likable," Beatrice added, "but normal."

Smith dug through Violet's things, apparently not caring that he was going through her bag while everyone was watching openmouthed. He seemed amused at the shocked looks on their faces. "Let's go through them then." Violet shook her head as Smith handed Beatrice some of Violet's paper and her favorite pen. "There's Mrs. Stevens. I think we can safely remove her from the suspect list."

Jack lifted his brows and then added, "Agreed. What

she said aligned with what Emily said. They have started looking into the family members, but all they've discovered is that Phoebe leaves her daughter with a girl near her rooms more than her husband realizes and that Harold lies about a business meeting every Friday at his work."

"Where does he go?" Violet asked.

"They haven't figured it out yet," Jack said, "just that his superior believes Harold has a regular appointment with a fictional client. For all we know, he goes to the pictures or the races."

Smith grunted. "If he's gambling, he isn't losing enough for it to show in their finances. He does all right for a newer fellow at his company. He's well-liked. He rents his rooms, but they're paid on time, and the woman who owns the building is quite fond of him."

"Is the woman also fond of Phoebe?" Violet asked.

Smith shook his head.

"I thought not. She was all right when we were shopping, but she's rather distasteful now. To be honest, I would happily never lunch with this old school chum again."

Jack laughed, but he wasn't that amused. "Murder turns the best of us into lesser versions of ourselves. I'm not sure your Phoebe started as the best of us."

Violet had no arguments with that assessment. Phoebe wasn't Vi's. They had the history of the same school and nothing more positive could be said of them.

"What about Phoebe?" Beatrice asked. "Are there any signs that she's the one who killed Olly?"

Everyone paused and then shook their heads. She was hateful, yes. Or she was upset and ready to lash out at whoever was around her, but there was proof of nothing other than she was dissatisfied.

"She's not gambling either," Smith said. "Outside of despising Delilah and irritating Vi—Phoebe seems like an unlikely candidate."

"As do the missionary and his wife," Beatrice said. "I was able to eavesdrop on them. The entirety of their conversation was about what their Christian duty was after this possible revelation. Stay home and support their family or return to the field."

"That only means that they didn't work together to killed Olly Rees," Violet said with exhaustion. "Whoever killed him is playacting his or her normal life right now."

Smith gave her a look of sheer approval which left Violet momentarily sad about the state of her being, but she decided to let it go. It wasn't her fault that people were monsters and she'd started to see it more clearly.

"What about the sons, did you find anything out about them?"

"I visited their houses earlier in the day," Smith said. "When I was getting the bread from the bakery."

"You got the bread?" Violet was surprised. She immediately followed that up with, "You did not."

"I'm a servant," Smith said righteously, "and the bakery was unable to deliver due to their auto being out of commission."

"Was that you?" Beatrice demanded. She expected the affirmative from her tone. "Did you ruin some poor baker's auto?"

Smith snorted. "It was convenient and I 'got lost' but even I don't have preternatural abilities. I just heard the housekeeper discussing it with the regular daily and volunteered to go. Regardless, both Edgar and Oliver have successful careers and nice houses. They're well liked in the community and timely on their bills from what I was able to learn. The worst that can be said is that Edgar sleeps through Sunday services and Oliver lets his dogs run wild. Both of their wives are well liked."

"They hardly sound nefarious," Jack said, and Violet yawned deeply.

"Why don't we split the family up and see what we can find out about them?" Jack suggested, eyeing Violet's yawn and his priorities shifted. It had been a long day with traveling, dinner, the drama after dinner, and then holding Mrs. Stevens as she wept. That did not, however, make Violet incapable of carrying on. She shot him a dark look and Smith cackled until Beatrice nudged him.

"Violet, you take Delilah," Smith said.

Violet shook her head. "I don't like her."

"Show her the picture you had taken of the twins," Beatrice said, "and then ask her for inane advice. The housekeeper said Delilah is obsessive over babies."

"But I don't like her," Violet said around another yawn. "Smith should take her since I barely like him."

"I don't like any of these people," Smith muttered without sympathy. "Mostly including you."

"You only like Beatrice," Violet said, unbothered. "Beatrice, you should look in on Phoebe and tell her that I sent you as a peace offering."

"She's not a slave," Smith snapped.

"She's an investigator who will probably end up mending loads of stockings," Violet agreed. "Feel free to take them and not do it. But perhaps you can compli-ment her and disparage me. I bet she'd love that."

Beatrice's gaze widened and then she nodded. She didn't look happy about it, but Smith did. "What will you tell Phoebe about Vi?"

Beatrice's unamused gaze moved over Smith, but he was impervious to her anger.

"I don't think you can do it," Smith said. "There's no way you'll disparage Vi even fictionally.

"I'll just pretend I'm talking about you and use feminine pronouns," Beatrice retorted just as another yawn came over Violet. She found that laughing and yawning at the same time were nearly impossible. She couldn't catch her breath because the choking was interspersed with giggles and by the time she'd gained control of herself, Smith had tugged Beatrice from the bedroom.

CHAPTER 15

*B*efore facing Delilah, Violet went to the bath, only to find the door closed. She started to knock but stopped when she heard a woman crying. Was it because of the murder of the grandfather or because she had murdered the man? Violet tried the doorknob and realized that it wasn't locked. Slowly, she opened the door. Charlotte looked up in horror. Violet held out the handkerchief in her pocket and the woman took it with shaking hands.

"I—I'm sorry. I'm monopolizing the bath, aren't I?"

Violet shook her head and sat down opposite Charlotte. "I'm sorry for intruding." She paused. "It's hard, isn't it? Losing someone you love?"

Charlotte nodded and then closed her eyes. This was a woman aching to pour out her troubles and Violet was the first sympathetic ear. "My husband doesn't want to stay here."

"England?"

"Here. Near my family. His is in the north. He says we should look to our families given our feelings since returning back to our country, but—but, he doesn't want our children around my family, and I can't blame him."

Charlotte shuddered with another sob as Violet sat next to her on the edge of the bath. She rubbed Charlotte's back as Vi would have done for one of her own friends. "Because someone in your family murdered your grandfather?"

Charlotte nodded, her crying only increasing.

"My cousin murdered my great aunt who helped raised us both." Violet's voice was low and sympathetic. Gentle even as she added, "I didn't do that. My brother didn't do that. Our other cousins, who we suspected for some time, didn't do that. Just her."

Charlotte looked slowly up.

"I still love the others and see the others. We exchanged letters and joys and spend time with each other as we can."

Charlotte dabbed her eyes as she sat straighter. Her voice was still tear-filled when she asked, "So you get past suspecting each other?"

Violet nodded. "I was the main suspect because I was the primary inheritor. They love me again. They loved me then."

"I love my family still," Charlotte said. "My husband says we need to abandon the sinners, but I don't want to."

"Well, they're not all sinners, are they?" Violet asked gently. "You aren't."

Charlotte's mouth firmed. "I don't want my children around the killer."

"Of course you don't. But I don't think there's more

than one killer. So the rest of the people you love are innocent."

Charlotte rubbed her brow and then blew her nose. Her spine stiffened as she gained control. "We have to find the killer. Before the rest of my family falls apart."

Violet was shocked by her instant liking of this woman. She set aside everything that was the periphery aside to focus on the primary issue. One of her family members was a killer, and the rest were being torn apart by that fact.

"Your family is full of believers, aren't they?"

Charlotte's face clouded. "You don't mean religious believers?"

Violet shook her head. "I mean believers that your grandfather was killed."

Charlotte closed her eyes again. "It's like a religious awakening. You just start noticing things. At first, they seem like nothing, but they add up to something powerful. Maybe something that can't be denied. Yes," Charlotte's face was sickly. "Yes, we're full of believers that Grandfather was killed."

Violet gave her a moment before continuing. "Your great aunt determined that it wasn't money."

Charlotte's eyebrows wrinkled, but she nodded. "Yes, of course it wasn't. My father keeps coming back to that. It wasn't money, but it was something."

Violet was gentle as she added, "And your grandfather didn't have enemies."

"He was a good man and a good patriarch. He was an honorable citizen. Why would he have enemies?"

"What would happen if there were a secret in your family?"

Charlotte took a slow breath in and let it out slowly. Her hands were trembling as she stood and washed her face. "You think that one of us had a secret?"

Violet nodded quickly. "Your grandfather was sharp in his mind?"

"He was," Charlotte agreed. "He was always observant and precise."

Violet lifted her brows at Charlotte and waited for her to finish.

"He might have noticed something. Perhaps that last day. He was fine in the morning. He joined me for breakfast with the children in the nursery and then we went on a walk together. He continued on when I took the children into the house. When I saw him again before dinner," Charlotte frowned deeply as her mind returned to that day. "He was upset. I'm sure he was. He didn't speak at dinner hardly at all which was quite unlike him. He loved to tell stories."

At some point over the course of the day, Violet thought, Olly Rees had noticed something with his children or grandchildren and it had affected his sleep, making him go for hot milk, and probably write in the missing journal. Whatever he'd learned had led to his murder.

Charlotte frowned as she tried to remember what had happened that day. "We were in those lagging days after Boxing Day and before New Year's. My husband joked that we didn't know what day it was or what we were supposed to be doing other than sleeping."

Violet nodded. She knew those days well. They were her favorite. Even before she'd married Jack and had a reason to linger in bed, she'd have lingered with a book.

It wasn't uncommon for her and Victor to lounge side-by-side playing checkers and leaving the floor before the fire covered in crumbs from too many sweets.

Charlotte rubbed her face. "It's different when you have children. You have to do more than sleep and eat. I was busy. The children were so excited after Christmas and a bit wild with too much sugar."

"Even Phoebe and Harold's daughter?"

"Alice?" Charlotte nodded. "Of course. She's quite little, you know. Barely two-years-old, but she was in the same nursery with my wild crew."

"Was Phoebe in the nursery with you?"

Charlotte nodded. "She doesn't like feeling as though she isn't beautiful or thinking she's overweight. She does like to goad poor Delilah, but Phoebe is more devoted than many a mother I've known."

Violet's mouth dropped open in unequivocal disbelief.

Charlotte laughed at the look on Violet's face before she explained, "It's not stylish to be a devoted mother. It's necessary to see Phoebe with Alice to recognize the love."

Violet didn't believe it. It was unfair of her, but in Violet's mind, Charlotte was projecting her own feelings about being a mother onto Phoebe. Rather than argue with Charlotte, Violet asked, "Who else was there that day?"

"Well," Charlotte said, frowning. "Everyone who is here now. Except for you and your husband and Miss Allen. My parents and uncle and aunt live in the local village, so they don't usually stay here during the day. When the family is around, they come for dinner and to spend time with their grandchildren, but why would they sleep here when their own beds are less than half an hour away."

"So they weren't here during the day?"

Charlotte shook her head. "Grandfather and I had the children with us and my parents don't come over during the day unless there is a reason to. All of us laying around, snoozing and eating isn't reason enough. I am almost positive they didn't arrive until just before dinner as usual."

Violet could see that so easily and her list of suspects narrowed to the grandchildren. The children of Olly Rees were Violet's least likely suspects anyway. Established themselves and with good foundations and no obvious motives, it was even harder to consider them when they weren't present when Olly was killed. If they didn't sleep at the house, then the suspects were their children. Reason enough, Violet thought, for them to say nothing when the doctor and the policeman assumed age for the reason of Olly's death.

Violet was willing to remove Charlotte and her husband as suspects, too, considering how long they had been away from the family. What terrible secret would missionaries from a remote location have to murder an old man? That left Joseph, his very quiet brother Alexander, Harold, and their wives. Violet immediately made Phoebe the villain in her mind.

"I HAVE A BIAS," Vi said as she flopped onto her bed while Jack adjusted his tie.

"Even I don't like Phoebe," Jack said. "I saw her

daughter try to run up to her today, and she stopped the child because she'd been playing outside. The child wasn't even dirty, she just could have been."

Violet winced. "We need to re-establish who the suspects are and what in the world was happening here."

Violet rose for her bag, digging through until she found the notes that Beatrice had made when they were home. She skimmed it and then started crossing whole sections out until it read:

Murder of Olly Rees

SUSPECTS:

Mrs. Stevens — Olly's sister. Was in attendance at the holidays and lives in Olly's house. Confessed to learning more about Violet and brought up the death of Aunt Agatha.

Mr. Oliver Rees— Olly's oldest son. Believed to have been in attendance at the holidays. Primary inheritor? Doesn't seem to have needed Olly's house. Father of Harold and missionary sister. Unlikely, he wasn't present during the hours that Olly discovered something about his family or when Olly was most likely killed.

Mr. Edgar Rees— Olly's other son. Believed to have been in attendance at the holidays. Did he inherit anything? Does he need money? Father of Joseph and other sibling. Same as above.

Harold Rees— Olly's grandson. Seems to have been a big fan of his grandfather and upset when it was suggested that Olly was murdered. Was he upset because Olly really was murdered? Or was Harold upset because the secret was out? Did he benefit from his grandfather's death?

Phoebe Rees— Olly's granddaughter-in-law. Seems to have liked him fine. No obvious reason for her to kill her grandfather-in-law. She and Harold seem to be doing fine financially from the outside. Are they really? Called her husband a snake in the grass. Was that because she was drunk or does she know something that others don't?

Joseph Rees— Olly's grandson by Edgar. Other than an heirloom surely he wouldn't be the primary inheritor. Seemed quite upset by the idea that Olly may have been murdered.

Delilah Rees— Olly's granddaughter-in-law. Why would she kill Olly?

~~Charlotte Rees- X — the Missionary Sister —Olly's granddaughter. At home during the holidays when she often wasn't. Did she benefit from her grandfather's death? Was it enough to push a supposedly religious woman to such a terrible crime?~~

Alexander Rees — Unmarried. What would a bachelor do over the course of the day, observed by his grandfather that would end in murder. Violet just couldn't imagine it.

~~Olly's friend who the earl spoke with— Believes Olly was killed as well. Is his saying so a ruse? A way to hide what he did? What possible reason could the man have for murdering his friend?~~

~~Who else was there?~~ Whoever killed Olly knew him well enough to know he was a sound sleeper, to know that a pillow would be available near his bed, to know that he wrote in his journal when he was sleepless at night. To know that the sheer fact that he got up for milk might just indicate he was troubled. He was killed by someone who knew him well and probably had something to hide that the old man had discovered.

QUESTIONS —

1. What was in the will?
2. Is Phoebe right that there wasn't enough money from Olly for anyone to murder him?
3. What are the finances like for the members of the Rees family? Is anyone in dire straits?'
4. Maybe it isn't about money. Maybe there was a murder, and it was about a family secret?
5. Did Olly know something that would have ruined someone's life? Is there a way to find out now that he's dead?
6. Did a doctor look at Olly's body after he died? If so, did they just assume he passed away? How was Olly found? Will the doctor talk to anyone? Perhaps Jack?
7. What did Olly discover about his family?

Violet looked at the last question and then underlined it. Just what had Olly discovered that was worth murdering someone over? Violet read the list over several times, telling herself not to focus on Phoebe and to think. Think about each of them individually.

There was Harold, who, Violet admitted, she didn't like all that much. But when she focused on the denizens of this house and left out the children, Violet appreciated only Mrs. Stevens and Charlotte. Harold, Violet focused. Who lived in London most of the time. Who would have a life very separate from his grandfather. Could he have some secret he wouldn't want the family to know that would come out to an observant man who was happy to have his grandchildren home? Did it have anything to do with those Friday appointments?

Violet frowned on that idea, muttering as she paced and nibbled her thumb. She was aware that Jack was watching her, but she didn't think beyond the comfort of his presence. While she paced Beatrice and Smith appeared.

Smith picked up the notes and read them over while Beatrice straightened the room.

"The letter," Smith said. "There was the start of that letter in his desk. The killer didn't know to look for that."

"The one to Joseph." Vi ran her fingers through her hair, dislodging her head piece and tossing it aside. Why had Olly Rees been writing to his grandson on the night he was murdered? Would it have been a plea to change his behavior? Would it have been a revelation of some sorts? A message about hunting the next day? It was impossible to say.

CHAPTER 16

*V*iolet's hand was on Jack's arm that afternoon as they entered the parlor to join the others for tea. They'd spent an afternoon of useless sleuthing reading through the accounts once again, attempting to see something in the family members and finding nothing and then speaking to Mrs. Stevens again who had no further incites to give.

As they walked into the parlor where the tea was being served, Vi's mind was still revolving with all the reasons that Olly might have been writing to Joseph. Her gaze fixed on Joseph. And his was fixed on his wife. She smiled up at him, full of love. Violet shook her head. Nothing to see there.

Vi looked for Phoebe and Harold. Phoebe's gaze was fixed on Joseph as well and there was a pitying disgust on her face. She placed her hand on her stomach, where her baby was growing, and then it moved to Harold where her expression smoothed into nothingness. Whatever Phoebe was thinking about her husband was entirely hidden.

Why was Phoebe hiding her thoughts? What did she know?

"Oh my heavens," Violet said, turning her face to Jack's shoulder to hide her reaction. As she did, her gaze met Charlotte's. Phoebe's gaze was considering as she looked between Delilah and Harold. Phoebe's gaze was masked, but her very attention drew Violet's to the others. To the duo she'd never considered together. Charlotte's gaze was as considering as it landed on her brother and her cousin-in-law.

Violet's gaze returned to Charlotte, and they were, both of them, wide-eyed with alarm. They were, both of them, thinking the same horrible thing. It seemed that being a missionary's wife and a woman concerned over the righteous choices did not prevent Charlotte from seeing what Violet-the-wolf had just seen.

Their gazes were locked and a silent, horror-filled back and forth. Violet let go of Jack's arm and crossed to Charlotte. They said nothing as they stared again at Joseph, then Delilah, Phoebe, and finally Harold.

"Not Joseph," Charlotte murmured low to Violet. "Not him. Look at the big lug."

"Not Phoebe," Violet whispered back. "She is one of the victims here."

"I—" Charlotte was sick as she stared at her brother and her cousin's wife. "No— It can't be him."

Violet wasn't going to argue with Charlotte. Instead Vi squeezed the woman's hand lightly and stepped back to Jack. Harold and Delilah. Harold and Delilah. Violet's gaze turned to Joseph and then to Harold.

But then Delilah said something to Joseph and he smiled at her, leaning over to kiss her on the forehead, and she leaned into him. Violet knew that move. It was one she did with Jack. He'd touch her and Vi would leaned in. She'd make his touch last longer and curl into him like a cat. It was not the move of a woman in love with another man.

Violet's gaze moved to Harold, whose mouth had tightened just enough. Now, he was a little jealous, Vi thought. She sighed and then glanced again at Phoebe. She shifted in her seat, full with Harold's baby, and all the while he was betraying his cousin and his wife. There was no proof, but Violet had seen many a cuckolding man and his lover before, she felt certain.

Violet imagined for a moment what it would do to her if Jack were to have done the same. But she couldn't imagine it. Jack was incapable of such a betrayal. He would never, ever do to her what Harold had been doing to Phoebe.

Violet turned to Charlotte as they accepted their teacups and whispered, "Delilah and Joseph? A love match?"

Charlotte nodded firmly and she looked as confused as Violet felt.

"It seems like it," Vi muttered.

Violet glanced at the cousins. They were clearly family. Their eyes were the same color, their hair was the same color, they came of the same grandfather, and one of them was betraying the other in a way that would ruin that relationship forever.

Violet focused on Delilah again, and when the woman glanced up, Vi smiled softly at her. Pieces fell into place. The love. The need for a child. The similarities in looks. By heaven, Violet thought, it was just obvious. She wanted nothing more than to set aside the earl grey tea for a strong cocktail.

Was this how Olly Rees felt when he'd made the connection? It was no wonder he couldn't sleep. And no wonder that his journal was missing. Where would they find it, Violet wondered. Would they? Or was it ashes lying in a grate?

When the tea was over, Violet hurried to her bedroom for the photograph of the twins and then went to see if she could find Delilah. Vi looked for a long time until she found Beatrice. Violet explained what she'd seen and then asked if Beatrice knew where Delilah had gone. "She's in the nursery. Be careful. Anyone who kills an old man is on the edge of madness."

Vi's brows lifted and she followed her former maid up the stairs and peeked her head in. Delilah was sitting in a rocking chair with a baby and Charlotte was holding a little girl that looked to be only a year or two old. The look of utter bliss on Delilah's face, knowing she couldn't have children, was painful to see.

Beatrice left as Violet entered the room, but Violet's business manager muttered, "You shouldn't be doing this alone."

Violet ignored the comment and introduced herself to the toddler, Alice, seated on Charlotte's lap. Alice shook Violet's hand and then giggled as Violet leaned over the baby Delilah was rocking. "What an angel."

Delilah's interlude was interrupted by Violet's nearness and the woman scowled at Violet before a look of adoration crossed her face again as she rocked Charlotte's baby. Violet looked at Charlotte, who was watching their best guess for the murderer hold her tiny baby. The baby was bigger than Victor's twins but not by that much.

"I have twin nieces, did you know?" Violet said sweetly to Delilah.

Delilah looked up and nodded.

"Would you like to see the photograph I had taken at Christmas? I knew a woman who loved babies as you do would be interested. I'm afraid Jack is rather tired of me blathering on about them."

Charlotte shifted silently but said nothing as Delilah leaned forward. Violet grinned at her and then said, "Let's exchange, shall we? I'm sure you can understand how I ache to hold a baby after Jack insisted we leave my nieces and return to London."

Delilah's gaze narrowed and Violet had to force herself to imagine something happening to her sweet nieces to make the sorrow fill her gaze in a way that Delilah saw and recognized. "He didn't."

"He did," Violet lied. "They feel like they're mine, you know. Since they're my twin's. And their mother is ill and they needed me, but Jack wanted to return to work."

Delilah carefully handed Violet the baby and took up the photograph. Her voice was low in wonder as she whispered, "They look just alike, don't they? What little angels."

"They are," Violet said truthfully, looking down at the baby in her arms. "What a sweetie."

"Oh, let me take her," Charlotte said. "She's got that look that says she's about to fuss."

Violet handed the baby over immediately and then leaned towards Delilah. "This one is little Violet, but we call her Vivi. And this is my sweet Agatha. Vivi, like her favorite aunt, is a bit of a hot-tempered thing. Agatha is pure angel."

Delilah was shaking her head as Charlotte handed her baby to the nanny and ordered quietly, "Take the children out. They need some air."

Delilah asked question after question of Violet while five children including Phoebe's daughter and the baby were gathered and taken from the nursery. The moment the door closed, Violet glanced at Charlotte who shook her head. It seemed she wanted her children well and truly away before they confronted Delilah.

When enough time had passed to calm Charlotte, she nodded at Violet, leaving the next step in her hands. Charlotte was probably uncertain of how to proceed. Violet felt as though one should approach it as if you were going to assault a person with a board.

Violet seamlessly shifted from talking about baby Agatha to saying, "It's because they look alike, isn't it?"

Delilah stared at Violet, confused. "Surely twins often look alike?"

"Not the babies. The cousins. They look alike. Joseph, Harold, Alexander, even Charlotte. They're so conveniently looking alike."

"Harold was the better choice," Charlotte said gently. "You wouldn't be ruining brothers that way. Harold and Joseph are as close as brothers, but they aren't brothers, are they? There's something sacred among siblings that you avoided."

There was no question that Delilah knew what they were talking about. She paled, stammering before she shook her head, but it was too late.

"How could you?" Charlotte asked. "Grandfather aside, how could you do that to Joseph? I thought you loved him."

Delilah bit down on her bottom lip as if fighting the need to reply. Her eyes rolled frantically and then Violet added, "It should have been obvious, really. When Jack and I saw you and Harold arguing in the park on the night of the scavenger hunt. No one argues like that if they aren't intimate."

Delilah was shaking her head and she'd bitten so hard on her bottom lip that it was bleeding. "No, no."

"But yes," Violet pushed. "You are. You chose a cousin, somehow convinced him to sleep with you, and you're trying to carry a child you can pass off as Joseph's."

"Joseph will never forgive you for Harold or for Grandfather," Charlotte accused.

Delilah stopped shaking her head and her sudden stillness was disturbing.

"He'll never forgive you. You ruined him, you ruined Harold, and you murdered Grandfather." Charlotte's voice was the cold, flat tone a mother used with her children when they were really in trouble.

Delilah found her voice. "Joseph will never believe you. He loves me."

"He will," Charlotte said, "when we explain it to him. It'll add up for him. Especially if he realizes if you left the bedroom. Maybe he's already wondered and shrugged it off."

"He loves me," Delilah snapped. "He loves me, and he knows how I sacrifice for him. And he'll never believe you because he's certain of my love for him and for the family we'll have."

Violet and Charlotte had been sure of Delilah's part in this before, but after that statement there was no going back.

Delilah's was a rather easy instrument to play when you knew where to hurt her, and it was without remorse that Violet added, "And, of course, no one will ever let you near their children again. They'll find out what a monster you are, and they'll pick up their babies and protect them from you. Just like Charlotte did already. She sent her babies away, and she'll never let you around them again. Phoebe will protect Alice from you. Harold might well lose them both. All because you drew him into your bed to steal a baby from him."

Delilah's unholy shriek of rage filled the air, and she lunged at Violet, clutching her around the throat as they both fell to the floor. Vi attempted to free herself, but it was like trying to shake off the grip of a gorilla. Charlotte was screaming hauling at Delilah, but it was useless. Violet gaped, struggling for air she could not reach.

Violet grasped Delilah's hands and dug her nails in. She gasped like a fish out of water, and no air got to her lungs. Her eyes were rolling in panic but the madness seemed to give Delilah a strength that Violet couldn't overpower. Finally, another pair of hands pried Delilah's vice-like grip from around Violet's neck and Delilah was pulled away, shrieking incoherently.

"You're a rabid wolf, you know," Smith murmured to Vi as he knelt next to her. "Beatrice is never going to forgive me. She told me to hurry."

Violet stared at him, holding her throat, and then her eyes welled with tears as she gasped painfully. A look of panic came over Smith's face as he took in the tears, and he bellowed, "Beatrice!"

CHAPTER 17

"This makes us even for the gunshot," Jack told Violet. The sick tone to his voice had Violet patting his hand. She tried to speak and croaked uselessly instead. He took her face between his hands, tilting her head to each side as he examined where she'd been choked. "Don't speak, Vi."

Jack had been mere steps behind Beatrice after Smith's bellow and when Jack found her holding her throat, he cursed deeply until Charlotte snapped at him. Jack cursed at Charlotte, then Delilah, and then pressed a gentle kiss to Vi's forehead.

"I'll call the police," Charlotte said.

"And the doctor," Jack and Beatrice ordered in unison.

Jack turned to Delilah again and found Smith had used his tie to bind the woman to her chair. Smith was entertained, Violet thought, and she went to say something sarcastic but she could only croak. That simply made the man grin before he smoothed his expression into politeness at Beatrice's disgusted look.

Jack cursed again. He pressed Violet closer and then kissed her brow. "We'll call the doctor, Vi darling. Don't try to speak."

His voice was a furious growl, and Vi had little doubt he'd be dressing her down with a sharp, terrified fury once he was sure she was fine.

Violet rolled her eyes at him, but his fingers were clutching her too hard. He had a hold of her as if he'd fight death for himself. He anchored her with his presence while Charlotte handed Violet a cup of chamomile and mint tea.

"I'm so sorry," Charlotte told Violet a moment later. "I'm so sorry this happened to you. I called the police and the doctor. If Jack will carry you to your room, you can rest until he arrives."

Before Jack could do more than let her sip the tea, the entire Rees family, led by Mrs. Stevens swept into the nursery, followed by Miss Allen and Mr. Baldwin. The nursery, which had felt cozy before, was now stifling.

"What is this madness?" Oliver Rees demanded, but he was overshadowed by the furious shout of his nephew, Joseph.

"Untie her at once!" Joseph demanded of Smith. "I'll have you drawn up on charges, my good man. How dare you tie up my wife?"

Smith simply arched a sardonic brow and nodded his head towards Violet. Joseph took in her blooming bruises and seemed unable to comprehend the connection between his bound wife and Violet's injuries.

"Joseph, he can't," Charlotte said gently. "Delilah killed Grandfather."

"She couldn't have!" Harold snapped. "It's not possible. How dare you say such a thing?"

"Oh," Mrs. Stevens said. She seemed relieved as she glanced about the room filled with her beloveds. Of them all to be the murderer, who was more preferable than the nephew's wife? It so easily could have been her own nephew or great nephew.

Joseph stared at his cousin and then slowly at his wife. He was shaking his head, speechless.

"She couldn't have," Harold repeated.

"Of course she couldn't," Phoebe shot out, but her tone was full of mean sarcasm.

"I assume," Charlotte snapped back, raking her brother raw with her judgement-filled gaze, "she did so because Grandfather realized you two were having an affair."

The family gasped at once and it seemed to be a near roar of choked horror. Harold jerked at the sound. When he saw their accusing expressions, he paled to a sickly green. Joseph spun on his cousin, grabbing him by the lapels, and demanded, "Are you sleeping with my wife?"

Harold gaped, striving for an answer. He failed.

"Of course he is," Phoebe said meanly. "Trailing his finger over her hand, along the back of her neck. A classic Harold move to ensure his lady is thinking of him." Her disgust was filled with fury. "I told you he was a snake in the grass, Joseph."

"Be quiet woman!" Harold snapped.

"No," Phoebe replied, calm for once. "You cuckolding

your cousin got your grandfather murdered. I'm surprised Charlotte and her husband aren't crying, 'Repent!' but perhaps they too believe there is nothing to be done for a man such as you. How could you do that? To him? To me? To Alice? You're a snake, Harold Rees. A betraying, no-good, nasty snake."

Her disgust had Harold taking a step towards her, but Alexander grabbed Harold's arm and in a low voice ordered, "Don't! You've caused enough trouble."

Mrs. Stevens and her nephews were watching the horror. Violet was surprised at the quietness, thinking her own family would be shouting. Instead, the reaction was just silent, judging eyes. The fathers were quietly conferring and Violet wanted nothing more than to hear what they had to say after such a revelation.

Mrs. Oliver had started to cry, turning into the arms of Mrs. Stevens while Mrs. Edgar crossed to Delilah and slapped her hard and vicious.

"Mother!" Joseph said, his voice cracking and his eyes wide with the feelings he was choking down. "Stop. Please stop. I love her. I love her."

Mrs. Edgar turned to take in Violet and then Mrs. Edgar's lips were trembling too. She crossed to Joseph, trying to hold him. He shrugged her off, and she moved back silently, holding her heart. Mrs. Oliver called to Mrs. Edgar, opening her arms and the two women seemed to collapse into each other.

Beatrice crossed to Violet and Jack and suggested that they come down to the bedroom and Beatrice would care for Violet. Jack started to carry Violet out of the room before the family argument turned vicious, but it was ended just as they left.

Mrs. Stevens slowly turned to her nephews and their family. "At least now we know."

Phoebe scowled. "We know and everything is ruined."

Violet would have liked to point out that Phoebe had known before and held it in, but Mrs. Stevens replied first. "It was ruined before. Now we can heal."

Phoebe's snort told them all what she thought the chances of that would be, but she was cut off from replying as the constables and doctor arrived.

While Dr. Welch helped Violet, the local constables arrested Delilah. Whatever family argument ensued among the relatives, they missed.

"What will happen to Delilah?" Beatrice asked Jack.

"She'll probably go to a sanitarium." He rubbed his hand over his face, and they all knew that the doctor was listening with interest.

Charlotte had left the family to attend Violet and she sighed. "That's for the best. She needs help."

"And Harold?" Beatrice asked Charlotte without sympathy for the killer.

The cuckold's sister winced and shook her head. "I don't know. Things can't really go back to the way they were before. It will take time for forgiveness and healing."

Violet imagined they couldn't. She rubbed her throat as the doctor checked her pulse again. Joseph clearly loved his wife. Vi wasn't sure that there would be forgiveness or healing between the cousins.

"And the journal?" Beatrice looked between Jack and Charlotte.

"It may never be found," Jack admitted. He ran his hand over Violet's back, still refusing to let go of her.

Every time he took in the forming bruises on her neck, he muttered darkly. "We won't need it given she attacked Violet. She might get away with the murder, but she'll end in the sanitarium for the attack."

Violet wanted to reply, but the doctor said, "Better not to speak, Mrs. Wakefield."

Violet would have ignored him, but Jack placed a hand over her mouth and handed her the tea.

"Don't speak for several days and see your regular doctor in London. Better to let your vocal chords recover, ma'am."

It was all tea and silence for Violet. Beatrice stood, glanced at Charlotte and the doctor, and silently began packing for both Jack and Violet. In mere minutes, their things were returned to their trunks and Beatrice had disappeared long enough to gather her own and Smith's things. Charlotte tried offering a continued bed for the night, but they were done with the Rees family, their home, and their murder. Despite the lateness of the hour, Violet was loaded into the auto with Smith, Beatrice, and Jack and driven home.

Right where she wanted to be.

The END

Hullo friends! I am so grateful you dove in and read the latest Vi book. If you wouldn't mind, I would be so grateful for a review.

THE NEXT BOOK in this series is available now.

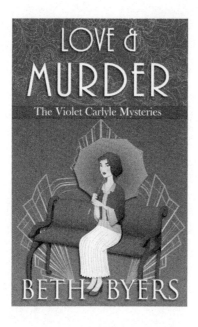

March 1926

On Valentine's Day, gifts arrived for Violet. Gifts that weren't from Jack. And they kept coming.

If she had to admit it, she'd say she was spooked. If Jack had to admit it, he'd say he was furious. If Victor had to admit it, he'd say the sender better run for his life. And soon.

Then they discover another woman received the same type of things. Gifts. Notes. Distant adoration. Only this woman has turned up dead. Trying to uncover the anonymous sender, Jack and Victor discover there isn't anything they wouldn't do to keep Vi alive and safe with them. It turns out there isn't anything Violet wouldn't do to stay with them.

Order Here.

THE NEXT POISON Ink mystery is also available for preorder.

April 1937

When Georgette Dorothy Aaron first started writing books, she little expected to effect real life. When she dives into writing crime novels with Robert, she little expected to see fiction come to life once again.

Once before she wrote a book and changed the fate of her neighbors. Was it happening again? Were the gods playing games with her? Or was she just noticing some-thing else occurring? Either way, another mystery is afoot.

Order here.

ALSO BY BETH BYERS

The Violet Carlyle Cozy Historical Mysteries

Murder & the Heir

Murder at Kennington House

Murder at the Folly

A Merry Little Murder

New Year's Madness: A Short Story Anthology

Valentine's Madness: A Short Story Anthology

Murder Among the Roses

Murder in the Shallows

Gin & Murder

Obsidian Murder

Murder at the Ladies Club

Weddings Vows & Murder

A Jazzy Little Murder

Murder by Chocolate

A Friendly Little Murder

Murder by the Sea

Murder On All Hallows

Murder in the Shadows

A Jolly Little Murder

Hijinks & Murder

Love & Murder

A Zestful Little Murder

A Murder Most Odd

Nearly A Murder

The Hettie and Ro Adventures

co-written with Bettie Jane

Philanderers Gone

Adventurer Gone

Holiday Gone

Aeronaut Gone

The Poison Ink Mysteries

Death By the Book

Death Witnessed

Death by Blackmail

Death Misconstrued

Deathly Ever After

Death in the Mirror

A Merry Little Death

Death Between the Pages (Coming Soon)

The 2nd Chance Diner Mysteries

Spaghetti, Meatballs, & Murder

Cookies & Catastrophe

Poison & Pie

Double Mocha Murder

Cinnamon Rolls & Cyanide

Tea & Temptation

Donuts & Danger

Scones & Scandal

Lemonade & Loathing

Wedding Cake & Woe

Honeymoons & Honeydew

The Pumpkin Problem

Printed in Great Britain
by Amazon

87861806R10099